Wakefield Press

HOMETOWN HAUNTS

Hometown HAUNTS

#LoveOzYA Horror Tales

EDITED BY POPPY NWOSU

Australian YA horror stories by

Wai Chim

Sarah Epstein

Alison Evans

Lisa Fuller

Margot McGovern

Poppy Nwosu

Michelle O'Connell

Emma Osborne

Emma Preston

Marianna Shek

Holden Sheppard

Jared Thomas

Vikki Wakefield

Felix Wilkins

Wakefield
Press

Wakefield Press
16 Rose Street
Mile End
South Australia 5031
www.wakefieldpress.com.au

First published 2021

Cover designed by Liz Nicholson, Wakefield Press
Cover and title page illustration by Jessie Brooke
Edited by Jo Case and Maddy Sexton, Wakefield Press
Typeset by Michael Deves, Wakefield Press

ISBN 978 1 74305 864 0

A catalogue record for this
book is available from the
National Library of Australia

Publication of this anthology was assisted by
the Commonwealth Government through the
Australia Council, its arts funding and advisory body.

TO ALL THE #LOVEOZYA
READERS AND WRITERS:
THIS IS FOR YOU, BY YOU

CONTENTS

Foreword

POPPY NWOSU

Dear reader,

Welcome to *Hometown Haunts: #LoveOzYA Horror Tales*. Within these pages, you will discover stories to thrill, excite, challenge and frighten you. I hope these tales get under your skin.

I've loved horror since I was a kid growing up in rural cane farming territory, when the very first stories that really stuck with me were the unsettling ones. It was always the books that I couldn't quite understand – those with unsatisfying endings and unexplainable events – that drew my attention over and over again.

Now that I have grown up, I realise how often horror is used as a mirror to reflect our times and enable us to piece together things that are difficult to understand. The world will always be bitter and sweet, beautiful and ugly, and the only constant is that our future is uncertain. This concept of the unknown is what this anthology is all about, a recurring theme that threads through every story.

So, for a new generation of Australian teens – who are growing up and coming of age in this current climate of uncertain health and environment, and interrupted daily life – I present you with a book to match the times. I hope it will leave you feeling unsettled, and give you the opportunity to ponder for yourself – what is it you fear?

The tales in this book – some scary, others weird, haunting or hopeful – are a reflection of the chaos all around us. Via these horror stories, our authors invite you to dig deep and see what you find. You may discover something unsettling and frightening. Or, by facing your fear, you may unearth something beautiful.

Poppy Nwosu

The Party

WAI CHIM

The thumping on my door comes with the same droning commentary I've heard all day.

'I'm so boooooored.'

I set down my book and take the shoddy headphones from my ears (ah, for the heavenly bliss of noise-cancelling). 'If you're really that bored, you could just practise a new way to say that. Maybe *I'm rather disinterested* or *I'm quite listless*?'

I anticipate the pillow Matt lobs at my head. 'Ugh. Why am I stuck in quarantine with the world's biggest loser?' he says.

I've been wondering the same thing. My plans for school holidays had mostly consisted of catching up on reading and some Final Fantasy raids. And while that hasn't really changed, I hadn't anticipated my brother's unrelenting presence. With our parents stuck overseas on a business trip after the borders were shut, my usual tactics of ignoring Matt's existence haven't been working that well. We actually have to do things together like buy groceries, take out the rubbish and enough basic tidying up so that we're not drowning in our own filth. After three weeks stuck at home, the situation is getting dire.

Remind me, for the next pandemic, to find a tidier quarantine mate.

'Seriously, I need to get out of here. Let's go to the skate park.'

And one that's less whiny. I glance out the window and then at the clock. It's already dusk. 'It's too close to curfew,' I say, shaking my head.

'Oh come on, Toby, you're such a goody-two-shoes. No one's going to stop us.'

'*You* go and explain to Mum how you copped a one-thousand-dollar fine.' I plug the headphones back in.

'Ugh. I'm going by myself. Loser.' His most unoriginal insult. I crank up the volume, let Adele's sultry sorrows fill my eardrums and go back to reading.

The shadows lengthen and peel away the last of the daylight. Matt's not back. And it's been longer than the allotted hour for being outside. I check my phone in case I missed something since it's always on silent but there are no notifications. The idiot really is going to get himself fined. I fire off a quick message.

Where r u?????

My stomach grumbles and I trawl through the near-empty cupboard for ingredients that could resemble food. As I'm rummaging through the pantry, my phone lights up on the countertop. I snatch it up, thinking it's Matt, but it's Mum and Dad checking in. They call twice a day from their Singapore hotel room. I angle my body to block the stack of cereal bowls piled onto the coffee table and check to make sure the ginormous pile of dishes is out of shot. Then I answer.

'Hey Mum. Hi Dad.'

'Hey honey. What are you – gosh not again!' Mum shouts to be heard over a blaring stereo. I catch the loud bass boom and slow riff and some foreign-sounding lyrics before the sound is muffled by Dad shutting the window behind her.

'Ugh it's been relentless,' Mum says. 'The kids outside have been blasting that song non-stop, some band that went missing overseas. It'd be tolerable if we could understand the lyrics.'

'*Say me, say me.*' Dad mock-sings the lyrics and Mum swats him.

'Don't do that, people will think you're making fun of them.'

I cringe at the racist undertones of my parents' comments. 'So, um, how's Singapore?'

'It's the same, we're in quarantine. So, you know. No curfew, so people are still going to the shopping malls every day, can you believe it? At least they're wearing masks . . . did you see in the US . . .?'

'Where's your brother?' Dad cuts in before Mum can go on her political rant.

'He went for a walk.' I do my best to keep my face neutral, but it's hard when you can see your own efforts in the corner of the screen.

'A walk? It's way past curfew,' Mum crows. 'Can that boy stay out of trouble? Why did you let him go?'

I keep myself from rolling my eyes. 'I'm not his babysitter.' *But it really is late. Where is he?*

'I should probably go,' I say. The last thing I need is my parents seeing me worry about my stupid brother.

'No pizza for dinner again,' Mum says as I end the call.

I rummage through the pantry looking for the pizza menu. My ears prick towards the door for the sound of a key in the lock but all I catch is the yowl of some tortured cat. *Where is Matt?*

Finally, my screen lights up with a notification. Typical Matt. He's sent a selfie. He's throwing a hang-ten, tongue out like a thirsty mongrel. But that's not what I'm gawking at – it's what's between his stupid tongue and his stupid hand. Big doe-eyes edged with thick liner gaze up at the camera behind animé-long lashes. Her glossy pink pout matches her bubble-gum-pink tube-top.

We're in the middle of a global pandemic, the whole city's in lockdown and somehow my brother is picking up girls at a party.

What the actual f??? WHERE R U????? WHO IS THAT?
You're SO DEAD.

My phone lights up again. More selfies with people. Everyone has dark hair and glossy-lipped pouts, even the boys. I peer closer. They're wearing high-end designer shirts, slim-fit cardigans, and blinding-white sneakers. Messy bedroom hair and fake tattoos scrawled across different points on their faces, which I assume is some trend. The pictures are too dark to actually make out words or letters, but I have to assume they're fake. Who would be silly enough to mark up such beautiful faces?

I'm not one to really focus on appearances, but even in my eyes, these kids are pretty. They're all East Asian, stunning and sophisticated next to my biceps-bulging, singlet-slinging, gym-junkie brother.

I'm boiling mad. Who *are* these people?? They're not from school and they're clearly not following social distancing and lockdown orders. They're having a PARTY, probably one of those ones where everyone's meant to catch Covid like the chickenpox.

My thumbs type furiously.

MATT YOU ARE SO DEAD. I CAN'T BELIEVE YOU WOULD DO THIS!! WHERE ARE YOU????

I glare at the screen, waiting for the three bubbles. Their absence infuriates me more by the millisecond.

A notification flag. Matt's sent a location drop. I squint at the blue dot among the tangles of faint grey lines. I look it up on Streetview: a nondescript single-storey house, just a few streets over.

I'm not sure what to do. It's after curfew and I've seen police cars driving around our neighbourhood. Their sirens are off, but I know they mean business. Like I told Mum, I'm not my brother's keeper. He's older than I am and he needs to learn to be more responsible.

But some part of me can hear Mum's disappointment. 'Matt can't help but get himself into hot water. It's his nature. You have smarts and a level head. That's why we count on you.'

Another notification flag. Another pic. Not a selfie, but a crowd shot. Matt is kneeling in front of their posed group. A line of smooth, perfect faces peer into the camera, their bodies slouched artfully. A sea of sensual, pouty lips.

And there's my brother's thick, slobbering tongue.

Ugh.

I sigh deeply and grab a face mask as I head out the door.

The streets are barren but bright, their houses lit from the inside. I imagine high-pitched laughter, buzzing reality shows, the sizzle and pop of dinners cooking, mingling to form a quarantine soundtrack. Despite the scariness of the pandemic, it's nice to know people are at home finding new routines, defining the new normal.

Except for me, out here tracking my idiot brother.

The blue dot is just in front of me now, but the house remains hidden behind a thick fortress of trees. I squint hard, looking for blinks of light. Listening for the pulsing thrum of music that would usually bring the cops to a party's door. But it's dead quiet. My scalp prickles. The sooner I find Matt and we can get out of here, the better.

And then suddenly I feel it, a deep boom bass, seemingly from nowhere. The sensation of it vibrates through my body, shakes my organs, drawing me in. I swear the street was silent just a moment ago, but now all I can hear is the music pulsing from inside as I walk up to the house.

The rest of the house is eerily still, no lights or people milling on the front lawn. Just this music that won't leave me alone. I head up the steps and go to ring the doorbell, but pause. What do I say? Do I take off my mask or keep it on? I'm not technically invited. How do you actually crash a party?

The door swings open wide and I snatch my hand back. No one is there. I do a double-take.

'Ahem.' I look down to see a petite girl, her hair in tight buns tied with ribbons. I would have mistaken her for a child, except for the thick eyeliner and heavy lipstick – oh, and what my brother would call her 'very stacked' chest.

She quirks an eyebrow but doesn't say a word. My mouth is dry and my voice comes out a bit croaky.

'Uh, I'm looking for someone. My brother.' She has one of those tattoos on her left cheek. Up close, I can see it's not words or letters but some kind of handwritten script, maybe Japanese kanji. There are four elaborately detailed characters, grouped together in a square.

The tiny girl half-rolls her eyes, but she steps back to let me pass. 'Um, thanks.' I'm on autopilot, my hands and feet all kinds of fidgety. This is the first time I've spoken to a stranger in weeks.

The hallway is dark, with the sort of furniture you'd expect in a grand mansion: plush velvet cushions, ornate feet under the chairs in the shape of paws. The withered boards creak beneath our feet. The music seeps from below, emanating like manic breath. The air is cool and damp. I hug my arms.

The girl leads me to a door. She swings it open. The music blasts, furnace-hot. But what hits me hardest is the smell. Rancid, sour, sulphuric. The gagging stench of rottenness gone rotten. I step back and bury my face in my arm. 'Ugh, what is that?'

The girl doesn't react, not even a shrug. She stands to the side, her tiny frame propping up the heavy steel in the doorframe. I gulp. Whatever this door is made of, however these walls are engineered and sealed, it's meant to be soundproof. *Whatever for? And why can I still hear the music up here?*

She jerks her head towards the party. The smell clogs my nostrils, lodges deep into the back of my throat. I can't go down there, no way. The girl jerks again. There's an unveiled threat in her stilted, unnatural movements. *I have to go.* I adjust my face mask, pushing down on the metal strip around the nose bridge, and step down into the bowels of the house.

The party is raging. Artificial smoke mingles with the stench, a moist hanging vape cloud. I push away the need to vomit and reach the bottom of the stairs. I'm in a monstrous room lit by crimson lights. The dance floor is crowded with swinging bodies. Their eyes are shut tight or unfocused, tilted towards the ceiling.

I step into the crowd. I'm not noticing the smell so much now, as if a fog has enveloped that part of my senses. Instead, I'm caught up by the sounds, the gyrations luring me into the space. I move and the world moves with me. At the few parties I've been to (Mum made me chaperone Matt), there were elbows and limbs flinging red plastic cups, dance-floor grinding, cliquey girls whispering and jocks trying to one-up each other in some dumb drinking game. There's none of that here. Just young bodies moving, writhing in sync, all mesmerising and beautiful.

What is this place?

A boy with the city's most chiselled jawline catches my eye. He doesn't smile but something in his expression is so inviting, knowing and hungry that I feel the heat climb to my cheeks. His face has the same tattoo. On him, it is exquisite. He tilts his head, drinking me in. A strange uneasiness creeps through me, like I'm suddenly naked. I hurry away, his eyes following me.

There's a little kitchenette in a cut-away wall. Matt could be here, getting a beer from a cooler or keg. But the fridge is empty. No snacks, no drinks, even the ice-cube trays are bare. The cupboards are empty too: no cups, no crockery.

'Looking for something?'

The boy from the dance floor has followed me. His words are a silky baritone with a distinguished accent, like a foreign diplomat's. His eyes dance with humour and his smirk reveals a dimple on his right cheek. I guiltily shut a drawer. 'My brother,' I stammer.

His smirk gets bigger. 'You won't find him in there.' My cheeks burn hot as he approaches.

'I— was looking for . . .' But I trail off, lost in the amusement of his eyes.

'It's okay. You're more than welcome to peruse. My home is your home. And let me know if you see something you like,' he adds with a wink.

He's flirting. He's actually flirting with me. My brain is a word-soup mess. For the first time in my life, I wish I had Matt's bone-headed confidence. 'Ah, this is *your* place?'

'For now, anyway, during this . . . situation.' He leans a toned forearm on the counter.

'The pandemic?'

'Do you know . . . *gangsi?*'

'What?' I ask dumbly.

He shakes his head. 'We're . . . travellers.' That intriguing smile messes with my senses. '*Tourists*, I think is the word. We were supposed to be on our way but . . .'

'The pandemic,' I say again.

'*Gangsi.*' *That word again.* I want to ask what it means but I forget everything when he leans closer. 'No matter. For now, we are here.'

'Oh so you're *all* living . . . here.' My heart relaxes a little. So they're a household, a really large household, but a household isolating together. It's not a Covid party at all. I guess that explains the smell . . .

'Ah well, *living* . . . might be a bit of a stretch.' He dials up the wattage of the smirk. He smells earthy and sweet. My thoughts jumble further. I can feel the energy coming off of him.

'I hope I'm not too forward doing this.' He reaches up

and pulls my mask down. 'It's just your face is so beautiful.'

I hold my breath, expecting the nervous cocktail of Covid, virus and quarantine to take over at any moment, but I feel eerily calm. He strokes my face with the back of a knuckle, a feather's touch.

'The tattoos . . .?' I ask.

He chuckles softly, still touching my face. 'You noticed those. Would you like one?'

'I . . .' I swallow hard. I can't tear my gaze away from his. Something in the back of my brain is screaming, but I can't make it out.

'What's your name?'

'Toby.' That comes out way breathier than I mean it to.

'Toby.' He says my name with harmonies and mid-notes. 'I'm Jin.' He offers his hand. I take it. It seems like the most intimate act ever.

'Hey Loser, you made it!' Matt's voice booms around me, like the voice of God. His forearm closes around my throat and his knuckles grind into my scalp. 'Dude, this place is wild! Can you believe it? I didn't realise they were setting up a Hype House here in Melbourne. So cool.'

His eyes dart to Jin, to our entwined hands. 'Hey, do I know you?' he asks him. I pull away and Jin laughs softly.

'I'm glad you're enjoying yourself. Please make yourself at home.'

'You bet.' Matt throws open the fridge. He frowns at its empty contents but isn't fazed. 'So give it to me straight, how does joining a Hype House work? Do you need a base first, or do you get picked and then you get to building your audience? I reckon I could get lots of followers if I wanted to.'

I grimace. This is Matt's dream, to live in one of those mansions with other testosterone-pumped teenagers doing dumb things for an audience. I've never seen him try so hard to impress a complete stranger before. Something about this place . . . or perhaps this boy.

Jin smiles knowingly. 'Please come, it's time to dance.' He places his beautiful fingers on my brother's shoulder and guides him towards the main room.

The music has been ratcheting up around us, the beat quickening. The bodies are all dancing, their bones jerking wildly, out of control, like puppets on strings. Jin leaves us to take a spot behind the DJ booth in the corner. Matt gets into the beat, raising his arms over his head. I sway a bit, feeling the energy of the music, but just watching the group around me. These beautiful, perfect bodies. Could this really be a Hype House collective? They sure look the part . . . even if no one is on their phones.

There are no phones.

A flash of pink as neon lights settle over Jin's soft features. The oversized headphones clamped over his head give him an ethereal appearance, alien but sexy. He catches my eye and throws me a wink.

The music fades to a soft hum and the lights flicker. The air around us electrifies, shifting us in a moment. The bass booms. It starts with a slow riff and a *one-two-three* . . .

Something is different about this song. I've heard it before. It grates my insides. The tune is catchy, the lyrics foreign but strangely familiar. I live in a pop-culture black hole, but I know this song . . . I know these moves . . . I know this group.

I heard it tonight. From Mum's call.

I turn to my brother to ask, but he's stone-stiff beside me. Then, without warning, he grabs my arm and in the dim, strobing light I can see his look of pure terror.

'We gotta go.'

Except we can't get to the stairs. The group is moving us, the swaying bodies herding us into the middle like we're sheep. I duck under some arms and try to push past but they've formed a wall of bodies. We can't escape.

'Forget this!' Matt lowers his head and lets out a guttural yell, charging forward like a bull. He smashes through the defensive line and keeps going, barrelling through until he crashes into Jin at the DJ booth. The giant speakers in front of the booth topple with a loud sizzle and pop. The feedback is excruciating. I duck my head and cover my ears. The music ends and the room fills with its absence. No one moves; the dancing has stopped.

Matt moans and pulls himself up. Jin is pinned beneath the equipment. The music is dead but the room is hardly silent. I can't tell if it's a trick of the room's red light, but as Matt makes his way back to me, everyone around us starts to change. Their faces droop, melting like candle wax, those pretty features pulling apart. They are not monsters, but certainly no longer human.

Bodies. We are surrounded by bodies. And instead of dancing, they are falling apart at the seams.

Matt and I catch each other's eyes. And we run.

The bodies leap out to stop us. Matt punches one in the face. The head snaps back, then rubber-bands upright on its neck again. I'm going to scream, but something is grabbing my leg. It's the girl who greeted me at the front door, but she's different now. That beautiful face has morphed into a flaking grey goop.

Her sneering teeth glow black and silver. The overpowering smell is back. I'm going to faint, but I have to *move*.

So I kick

and kick

and kick

and kick out.

And I'm free and stumbling up the stairs, right on Matt's heels, the creatures close behind.

My lungs scream when the fresh air hits. We run and run until I can't run anymore.

'Stop. Wait,' I say. 'They're not chasing us. I don't think they can leave the house.' I gasp and lower my head between my knees, wheezing to catch my breath. Matt jogs back to me.

'What the hell was that?' I gasp, when I can manage words. My mask dangles from one ear.

Matt is on his phone. For a second, I think he's calling the cops, which reminds me of curfew. I'm back to the reality of quarantine. *What was that back there?*

My brother's face is as white as his singlet. His hands shake as he hands over his phone. I peer at the article he's pulled up.

The feature image is too familiar. The beautiful figures slouched artfully in a row. It looks like the selfie Matt sent me, but without my brother in it. Their cheeks are unmarked. No weird tattoos. In the middle: the smiling, smirking, perfect Jin. I swear his picture winks.

The caption dates the story accompanying the image to four weeks ago. I read the headline.

BELOVED ICONS ASSUMED DEAD:
KOREAN POP GROUP MISSING IN AUSTRALIA

Seek and Destroy

JARED THOMAS

Dave wound the bulldozer engine down to silence.

'Bradley.' I looked up, and he was waving me over.

He climbed down from the vehicle, and I walked over from the shade of one of the few gum trees along the section of the big, wide creek, stepping into the blaze of the forty-five-degree midday heat.

We looked at the scoop he'd cut out of the earth, the moist layers beneath the cut. And the brittle bones laid out before us. Shitloads of them.

'Jesus,' I said under my breath.

'Jesus, alright,' Dave muttered, pulling up his shirt to wipe a stream of sweat from his face. He looked up the creek. 'Well, it's a good thing they've pissed off for a while.' He gestured to the Aboriginal people monitoring the excavation, visible in the distance in their hi-vis shirts, fitted out by the company.

'They'll be back in twenty or so, maybe I better go and warn them?' I said. There's no way I'd want to stumble across the bones of my ancestors, freshly ripped from their graves.

'Here's trouble.' Dave said as the big-time construction manager's land cruiser pulled around the bend. *Cyril.* As if we weren't in enough trouble already.

He got out of the car and walked toward us, wearing slacks, a shirt and polished boots, like a real goose. Dave and I trod carefully in and around the bones.

'Maybe these are just goat bones?' I said. It wasn't a far stretch of the imagination – there were always goats walking along the ridges of the hills that towered over both sides of the creek.

We didn't even need to say anything to Cyril. He just punched his fist into his thigh.

'Jesus! Just what we bloody need,' he said.

'It's not very Catholic of you to speak that way, Cyril.' Old Dave seemed to be trying to alleviate the seriousness of the situation.

Good Catholic boy, my arse. From what I could tell, Cyril was just a self-entitled, nasty prick whose talent was ordering people around.

He'd told me he was doing me a favour getting me out on the site, but who else other than the trainee was he going to get to stand around with a few blackfellas, in forty-five-degree heat, watching an old man go up and down on a front-end loader and grader? If I'd known my days were going to be spent like this, there's no way I would've tried so hard at school.

I turned to look at Cyril and his flash boots getting dusty, and then he declared, like he actually believed it, 'They're just goat bones. Look, they're everywhere.' He pointed at the goats straddling the ridges. I'd said it, too. But I was just trying out the idea. Listening to the words come out of Cyril's mouth, it was obvious they were bullshit.

Dave lit a cigarette. 'The problem is, Cyril, it's going to be as plain as day to the blackfellas walking back up the creek that these bones don't belong to goats.'

'They're goat bones,' Cyril repeated, more of an order than a statement.

Dave took a drag on his cigarette and exhaled into the swelter.

'Well, I'll leave you to explain to them why that skull there is missing a pair of bloody horns.'

Cyril paced up and down, hands folded over his head. I didn't want to look at the skull, but couldn't help catching a glimpse of the nose socket full of soil.

'Just grade back over it,' Cyril ordered, as if his solution was reasonable.

'But they're still going to see what's there when we dig down to the level.' Even as the words left my mouth, I realised Cyril wouldn't appreciate the trainee speaking up.

He lowered his hands to his hips and looked along the creek. 'Dig another hole up there, out of the construction zone, then bury them there.'

'We can't do that,' Dave said, stepping on the butt of his smoke.

'We're going to have to! We can't afford for this work not to go ahead! Or have you got a few other multimillion-dollar contracts lined up, Dave?'

Reluctantly, Dave pulled his big old body up on his rig. I sat back down in the shade and lit a cigarette. Cyril walked over to the spot where he wanted everything buried.

As I waited in anticipation for the old Aboriginal people to come back and blow the whole scene apart, I thought about what my lawyer cousin from the city had told me at Christmas lunch. She reckoned that none of the Aboriginal folk wanted any construction to go ahead, and they were only approving it because their native title or whatever didn't offer them any protection. The most they could hope for was a few bucks to look after the remaining little bits of their country they had control over.

The old people, two men and a woman, hadn't had a whole lot to say before they'd walked down the creek. It wasn't too hard to tell they weren't entirely happy with what was going on. I mean, if it were my home, I'd want to be protecting it too. I'd learned at school that this place was billions of years in the making, and that the small pools of water below the ranges were a miracle in our dustbowl of a place.

The Aboriginal people had picked up stones when the grader exposed the top layer of earth. 'Just want to make sure they're not the tools of our old people,' they told me.

But the morning had gone smoothly, so I guess that and the heat beat them into feeling it was safe to go for a stroll to find some shade and a waterhole.

Cyril, hands on hips, waved Dave towards him, as if the old man didn't know where he was heading. I had no sympathy for Cyril and the company we were working for.

There'd been protests. Not just the blackfellas, but the greenies, and even regular old town people. A big mob of them had barricaded Woolworths.

Blood Money, one of the placards read. *Not your precious metals to sell – It's our precious land*, another sign read. Among the protesters, a big, tall Aboriginal woman had raved about how the mining site was sacred.

And then this old Aboriginal bloke, dressed in a collared tee, an Akubra hat and a pair of moleskins had started yelling at the Aboriginal woman. 'Shame on you, there's people in this town who need the work! There's been no work here in years. Who are you to stop people from having a good life?'

And she started yelling back, 'I'm a T.O. here,' (which I later learned means Traditional Owner), 'and you've got no shame talking on my country. You're as bad as them money-hungry mob. But this country knows you, it knows you should know better! This country going to make you pay, the spirits of this country going to get you if you let anything happen.'

I could still hear her screams the next day, as I read an article in the local rag about the old Aboriginal bloke speaking up to the protestors. A member of the town council, he reckoned he wanted to see both blackfellas and whitefellas getting work in the town. He must be about the age of my grandad, and he talked about how sad it was that people couldn't get work like his generation could. How with a drought on, the rare minerals mining venture was as good as rain.

'People shouldn't be protesting about mining rare minerals when they're using their laptops and phones made of rare metals to protest and look at porn,' he'd said, as if protesting and porn were the same thing.

The hole was dug, the bones had been buried, and a layer of topsoil had been placed over the area where the bones had been found by the time the monitors had returned. Dave was grading another section of the creek, where the bulk of the sorting plant would be built.

'Nice stroll?' Cyril asked the Aboriginal people, as if nothing had happened.

'Yeah, deadly,' said the old woman, Denise, as goats rushed down from the range and onto the creek bed behind her.

'There was wildu up there, a couple of them circling around,' said one of the old fellas, Charlton.

'Eagle hawk,' explained the other old fella, Barry, seeing me try to figure out what his brother had said. He turned to him, saying, 'the kutnyu yakati don't know yura mityi,' which I think meant something like, *the dumb-arse white kid doesn't know Aboriginal language.*

I looked up at the sky, and so did Cyril. Seven massive eagles were circling directly above the site where we found the bones. I looked away. The goats kept moving towards us, as if they wanted to hear the conversation.

'Yeah, those eagles, they're the kings of the sky,' Denise said. 'They see everything.'

My stomach flipped. It was a good thing it was forty-five degrees or Cyril would have to explain why his pink face had flushed red.

'How about we call it a day?' he suggested. 'It's a bit dangerous in this heat. You'll still get paid a full day.'

The monitors looked at each other, as if entertaining the offer. Barry looked over at Dave on his grader.

'We better see what that fella is up to first. Our ancestors and the spirits don't have a knock-off time for us.'

And then all I heard was the goats bleating, about twenty of them, as if they were trying to blow our cover. I wanted to pick up one of the big rocks from the creek bed and beat the goats into silence.

Cyril and I walked with the monitors up the creek, away from the site of the disturbed grave. When we arrived at the site the bones had been moved to, the monitors started turning over stones and things.

Charlton picked up a bone.

Jesus. Dave switched off the grader and Cyril shuffled around, looking like he was going to shit himself. Dave climbed down from the grader, and the three of us walked closer to get a look.

Charlton held out the bone: the hoof of a goat hanging to it by a thread.

'We shit ourselves,' Barry said.

'Oh Jesus,' Cyril laughed. I don't know if it was the stress of it all, but Dave and I started belly-laughing too.

'We thought it was one of our old people,' Denise said, and then we all stopped laughing.

'Had enough for today?' Cyril asked.

The monitors looked around. The land stopped breathing. All was silent. And then two black swans flew towards us, making me jump out of my skin. I watched them skim above the ancient creek bed, their wings flapping a hundred miles an hour.

'Yeah, I reckon,' Barry said, watching the swans. 'Not much to go now, hey?'

'Not here anyway,' Cyril said, looking around the site and then up to the top of the ranges. 'Tomorrow, we'll move on to the excavation areas up there.' The seven eagle hawks were there now, turning their threatening circles.

I jumped into the four-wheel drive with Dave. We travelled back into town in the rear of the convoy, dust kicking up everywhere.

'God knows how we got out of that one?' Dave said.

'I wasn't trying to get out of anything.'

'You'd be out of a job if construction was held up any longer.'

Yep, I had to keep remembering what everyone was telling me. *I was lucky to have a job.*

'But don't you think we should say something?'

'They went for a walk when they were supposed to be monitoring. I was following Cyril's directions. They didn't know those bones were there. I don't think it's going to mark the end of the world for anyone if they're moved a little down the road.'

I shrugged, thinking about what Barry had said about ancestors and spirits not having a knock-off time.

The first time I'd heard blackfella talk about spirits was when I was on Year Five camp at Rawnsley Park in the Northern Flinders Ranges. I had to share a tent with this fat kid, Benny, and an Aboriginal kid, Victor Rempy Victor was a foster kid, tough as guts, always talking about breaking into cars. Benny kept ripping disgusting farts that smelled like a can of dog food combined with crusty sneakers, so Victor decided to start winding him up.

'You fart like that, fat Benny, and the kutnyu come get you.'

'What?' Benny asked.

'The spirits.'

'What spirits?'

'They're everywhere.' Victor turned on the torch and shone it up at him. 'There's some fellas, they had their guts cut with rock, and coals shoved inside of them, and they full of fire, their eyes are fire, and they can't be touched by nothing. And then there's just ghosts, like whitefella ghosts, but I could call these fellas here right now if I wanted to. There's all kinds of different spirits out here,' he said.

'You're full of shit,' Benny said.

Victor grabbed a fistful of Benny's pyjama top and he growled, 'Don't risk it, they can hear you! They're everywhere. You do the wrong thing, they mess you up.'

'Okay, okay!' Benny said and he lay back down, probably thinking that Victor was going to whack him. 'I won't fart no more.'

All I could think about was the fellas with coals inside of them as I heard what I hoped were emus cruising around in the bushes.

'Hey Victor,' I said, 'those spirits have a name?'

'There's kutnyu. That means ghost.'

'Right,' I said, 'but do they have a name like Rambo or anything like that?'

'You bloody been listening to me or what?' He shone the torch back in his face, the shadows catching all of his scars.

'Maybe I missed something.'

'Right. Well there is this one bloke . . .' He dropped to a whisper. 'Georgie Barnes.'

'Georgie who?' Benny asked, and then Victor actually did whack him in the side of the head.

'Don't say his name too loud! If he hears you, we're gone . . . us, this tent, everyone else around us.'

'Okay, sorry!' Benny said.

'Don't say his name again. You're lucky to say it once and not get taken.'

We all lay back down again. I knew that fat Benny was absolutely shitting himself. I mean, I was shitting myself, and Benny was a sook.

'But Victor, who is that fella, the one you can't talk about?' Benny asked.

'Bloody white boys, always asking questions.' Victor shone the torch back on his face and leaned on his side. 'He was a carver. He carved the best spears and boomerangs. And he was the best hunter, and he was warrityi, emu man. When whitefellas came, they killed him with guns, and because of that, his spirit is really pissed off. He couldn't understand why his spears weren't as deadly as guns. If you do something really bad, boy, it's Georgie Barnes that comes after you.'

'You said his name,' I whispered, jumping as he said it.

'Yeah, but I haven't done anything wrong. Have *you*, boy?' Victor said.

I lay in bed frozen, thinking about all of the bad things I'd done in my ten years on the planet.

Victor interrupted the silence. 'Georgie Barnes comes after you, and he gets the spirits before him to help, and they call on the spirits before them to come. And if he can't find you, he comes after the person you love.'

I thought about the person I love most, Grandad, and shivered.

'Been an interesting day young fella, you want a beer?' asked Dave, just before he pulled over to drop me at my car.

I barely had enough money for a glass of water but I knew Dave would shout me a beer.

'No worries.'

'I'll meet you at the Tavern.'

I jumped in my ute and switched on the stereo. I've had Metallica's *Kill 'Em All* stuck in the CD player since the day Grandad gave me his old ute. I needed something to take my mind off things. And I didn't want to hear the V8's engine, which had been skipping a beat. I didn't want to hear it until payday, at least.

Seventy clicks and a corrugated dirt road, sand dunes, the occasional mallee and a whole lot of saltbush lay between me and town. I stared at the tailgate of Dave's truck, thinking about the blackfellas. To say I felt bad about not telling them what we'd unearthed was an understatement. *Who gives a shit if they were taking a walk down the creek? It was probably the first time they'd been onto that country since we screwed them over.*

The hammer and noise of 'Whiplash' was doing a good job of distracting me until a sting pulsed at my chin. I pulled down the sun visor and looked in the mirror. Another zit ripening. I pinched my fingers on either side of it, ready to squeeze . . . And then an emu bumped up next to me, sending the ute almost onto the verge. *What the hell?* I looked at the speedo. I was doing seventy-five clicks. *Not possible.* But the emu kept thumping into the car, as hard and fast as the drums on the stereo, and I had to keep pushing back against it to keep driving in a straight line. And then two more emus were banging up against me on the other side of the ute, with the force of an army tank. *Thump thump thump thump.*

Piss off! I put my foot down, just enough to almost kiss up against Dave's bumper, pulling away from the emus and their battering. When I looked back, the emus were nowhere to be seen. Nowhere. The only battering to be heard was inside the car, on the stereo.

When we pulled into the car park out the back of the tavern, I checked my door. No extra dings, no scratches. Nothing.

We made our way through to the pokies. An old black woman sat at one of the machines, dropping in bucks. She looked up at us as we approached. And then she sprung up from her chair. She seemed too old to move so quickly. She pinned her back up against the machine and looked at us like we were pointing a gun at her. I looked away, looked back and she was tearing off out of the Tavern.

She bloody knows.

The old Aboriginal fella at the bar must have known too. He gave us the same look, then took off through the nearest door, leaving his half-finished beer on the bar.

'What the hell was that about?'

'What?' Dave asked.

'The old woman in the pokies, the fella who was drinking that beer.' I nodded in the direction of the pint.

'Protest,' Dave said, straightening my collar, 'you're wearing your Marked Metal hi-vis, mate.'

I stuck around with Dave for a bit, had a couple of pints, enjoyed the aircon and the barmaid's pouty mouth. In any other town you'd have to worry about being done for drink-driving. In this town though, a young fella in a Marked Metal shirt didn't have to worry.

I got home, said hi to Mum, grabbed some food, nodded at

Dad, went out to my granny flat, cracked open a can of beer, and flicked on the box to watch some mind-numbing shit to take my mind off things. It took me another couple of beers before I crashed.

I switched on the radio as I made my way out of town back to the site. There was a report about the black councillor dying in suspicious circumstances. All that was reported was that his car had come to a halt after hitting a light post on the northern end of the bridge crossing the gulf.

I needed a cigarette but I was out of papers.

I looked at the fluoro tape along the side of the battered bridge fence as I crossed it and pulled up at the servo just north of the bridge.

'Papers,' I said to the bloke behind the counter.

'Did you hear about the black councillor?' he asked as he turned.

I just nodded. I didn't want to hear bugger all. But in a town where nothing happens, every man and his dog are keen to tell you a story.

'I know the bloke who was driving behind him when it happened. He veered up against the bridge fence, and my mate thought he was going to go off the edge. Then he veered back into the middle of the road. The car hit the fence on the other side, came to a stop. My mate jumped out and found the old bloke with a boomerang through his throat, pinning him to the headrest. Even weirder though: the car windows were alright. None of them were smashed.'

I took off from the servo and tried to make sense of what I'd just heard as I rolled a cigarette. I could hear the screams of the protestor out the front of Woolworths again: *This country going to make you pay, the spirits of this country going to get you, if you let anything happen.*

As I drove back out to the site, I decided to listen to my V8's missing beat, hoping it would distract me from the scenarios running through my mind.

'Should we wait for 'em?' Dave asked after our third cigarette.

I just shrugged. I didn't want to think about it.

'So what are we going to do? You heard from Cyril?'

'Nah, I'm just the trainee. Let's just see if we can get the machinery up the ridge, I guess.'

Dave nodded. We drove around the creek bend and into the valley, to the grader and front-end loader. I spent the next few hours walking in front of the loader, up the range, observing Dave guide tons of metal up and over impossible rocks at impossible angles. The eagle hawks soared above us the whole time, as if they were going to swoop at any minute. They looked strong enough to lift me up and carry me away.

A northerly wind was picking up. From the range, I could see red dust kicking up on the plains.

Dave parked the loader at the excavation spot, and looked over to me. 'Well, I guess it's time to wobble down the hill. There's fish to be caught.'

I wished he'd ask me if I wanted to head out fishing with him. I was broker than the day before and watching the cricket on TV was the only thing going.

Dad woke me up. 'What the hell?' I sat up and tried to straighten myself out. Dad hadn't stepped foot in my room in years.

'I'm sorry mate.'

'What?'

'Old Dave.'

'What about him?'

'He died.'

'How?' I asked, snapping into gear.

'You don't want to know.'

'Yeah, I do,' I said, eyeing empty beer cans on the bench behind Dad.

'He was found in a mess on his boat. It drifted back in to shore. One of the shack owners found him.'

'What type of mess?'

I watched Dad's face contort. 'His face was torn off, mate.'

'By what?'

'His boat was full of emu feathers.' Dad patted me on the shoulder. He stood awkwardly, as if he was about to say something else. But he didn't. On his way out, he saw all the empties and shook his head.

I thought about calling Grandad. I wanted to warn him not to go fishing, but he'd think I was crazy.

'Bradley,' Cyril said when I picked up the phone. 'Did you hear about Dave?'

'Yeah.'

'Sorry mate, but we've got to get on with it. I'll meet you out at the site. I've got another driver.'

Bugger this shit. I pulled on my boots and then slipped my tobacco into my back pocket.

A dust storm was blowing towards me as I drove off the

bitumen and onto the dirt track to the site.

I could see it up ahead: Cyril's vehicle skewed in the middle of the road, about fifty clicks out of town. It was like a magnet, drawing me to it. *Turn around*, I told myself, but I pulled up about a hundred metres from it. I walked towards it as fast as my steel-caps would let me go – a snail's pace. I was in no hurry, anyway. The northerly wind blew dirt up against my legs.

The motor of Cyril's vehicle was running. Idling. I walked up to the driver's side. There were massive dents in the door. I couldn't see Cyril. I just wanted the ignition to switch off. It was driving me insane, its humming in the middle of the bush.

I opened the door.

Cyril and the other bloke, the new driver, were slumped over the console, clubs embedded in their skulls. Aboriginal clubs, wooden, soaked in blood.

'Noooooo!' I screamed as I ran back to my car. To my left I could see the emus on the plain, about five of them, swinging their attention in my direction.

I dived into my car and put my pedal to the metal. When I slowed down and straightened up, my ute started snaking. I looked in my rearview mirror. The emus were chasing me. Behind them, three massive whirly-whirlies were spinning towards town.

I fanged it, feeling the wind – and something I didn't understand – breathing down my neck. When I looked again in my rearview mirror, the whirly-whirlies seemed to have petered out.

I grabbed my tobacco and rolled a smoke. As the tobacco hit my bloodstream, I realised I'd have to tell the cops about Cyril. And then the car jolted forward, as if my engine had been injected with adrenaline. I glanced at my rearview mirror. The whirly-whirlies, towering over the ranges, were gaining on me.

My phone rang and I scrambled to answer it.

'Young fella,' came the voice down the end of the phone.

'Who's this?'

'It's Barry.'

I froze. 'How did you get my number?'

'Your dad's the carpenter, so was your grandfather, and your great-grandfather. You're not that hard to track.'

'What's up?' I asked, trying to sound calm.

'I was calling to ask you the same thing. Is there something you're not telling us, boy?'

'I wanted to te—'

My phone was bumped out of my hands as a wave of red dust hit the car.

Grandad was all I could think about. He'd be buggered if the wind hit him out on the boat.

I took the route around town for heavy vehicles, around the salt lakes, lined by bush. The temperature indicator read fifty-five degrees. *Impossible.*

I noticed how bright it was, storm clouds gathering over the ranges, and my ute's engine still missing that beat.

I switched on the stereo. It might help. The killer guitar riff kicked in, then the drums built, and the bass started pushing the song along. Then – 'ALRIGHT!' screamed James Hetfield. 'Seek and Destroy'.

I almost jumped out of my skin. *Bugger that.*

I went to turn the stereo off. It wouldn't. The car pounded with music. I kept hitting the off button. Then I started punching it. Nothing. James Hetfield's singing continued. And then I was swallowed by a sea of red dust. Branches flew across my bonnet, then a tree, then another, its roots cracking my windshield. The stereo's volume started turning up, up, *up*, to full notch.

I shot past the turn-off to Grandad's and pulled on the hand brake, sending the car into a spin. I snaked back onto his road.

And James Hetfield kept on singing about running, hiding, paying, dying . . . *Seek and Destroy.*

I almost collided into Grandad's front door when I skidded to a halt. His boat was blown off the trailer, the back of it banging against the ground. His Harley was on its side.

I barged through the door.

Grandad was sitting beneath the aircon, watching the cricket, the volume down.

He looked at me like I was cooked. 'How you going, Brad?'

He raised his glass of whiskey, grabbing his beard before taking a swig.

I could hear my breathing as I looked at the Aboriginal artefacts surrounding his living room. The spears pinned to the wall, the boomerangs on shelves, the clubs on his coffee table.

'Grandad, why do you have all this shit?' I asked as he focused on the cricket. I heard the clock ticking, felt the cool of his aircon. The house was almost silent, apart from the ticking of the clock, my breathing, his scuffles.

'What shit would that be, Bradley?'

'The Aboriginal stuff.'

He gave me a long, hard stare like I'd lost my mind. Then he turned his attention back to the cricket. 'Better to have Georgie

Barnes on the inside than on the outside.'

One of the boomerangs moved. I swear it moved. Just an inch. Then quivered. 'Who?' I asked, my voice breaking.

'Georgie Barnes.'

'How do you know about G— him?'

'My grandfather, your great-great-grandfather, used to call all the natives Georgie Barnes. Got no idea why.' He swivelled his armchair in my direction.

His eyes widened. Looking at me, but past me. I twitched a shoulder, ready to turn and see. Then – '*ALRIGHT!*' – Metallica blared through the walls. A spear passed my hip and pierced Grandad's chest. Blood spouted from his lips.

'Run,' he mouthed.

It's Quiet Now

EMMA PRESTON

The beginning of the year 2020's lockdown was a weird time for everyone. During this time, I was at university and still had classes to attend before the full lockdown. I remember walking around the city. It was quiet, and no one was around. But I still felt like I was being watched. It reminded me of when me and my family went camping out in the Flinders Ranges, which became the inspiration for this story.

As the lockdown begins, the cities grow silent.

Monsters who fear noise take solitude within the unpopulated areas of the Australian outback. But when people start to lock down, and cities and residential areas become quiet, these curious monsters decide to do some investigating. When the lockdown ends, however, streets become bustling once more and the monsters take refuge in alleyways.

Most leave, deciding that the noise is too much to bear. But some stay, having adapted to their new existence.

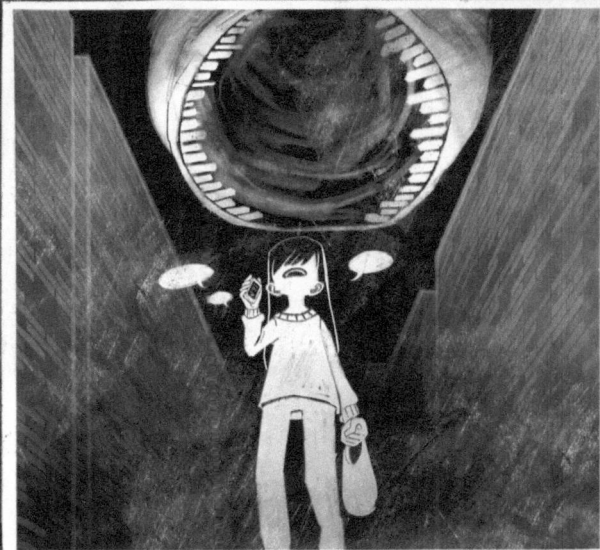

Heart-shaped Stone

VIKKI WAKEFIELD

Arlo eases the screen door shut on its creaky spring and slips a jacket over her pyjamas, boots on her feet. Summer has ended and nights are getting cooler; for the first time in months the family slept with closed windows and doors. It's still dark, with an eerie yellow glow rising east.

She gathers her egg apron and a torch from the porch cupboard and makes her way along the stony path to the roost. The dogs slink reluctantly from their burrows under the house: four of them, all different sizes, colours and breeds, one missing an eye, another a tail. They came with no names. The Shepherd is boss; he falls in at Arlo's heels, stretching and whining, and the others follow at a respectful distance.

Behind her, a light flickers on and the generator starts up. A sheen of condensation slicks the tin roof of the roost. She unlatches the gate and squeezes through, careful not to let the dogs get a nose in the gap. They've learned to share scraps, to keep clear of snakes, roos and boots, but Uncle made the mistake of tossing a dead chook into the yard once, and this lot have forgotten their manners.

Uncle takes the ones nobody wants. Dogs, cats, cows, sheep, horses – missing this or that, busted or poorly healed bones, bad genes, rotten temperaments, or just plain ugly. He gives them a good life until it's their time, and then it's one final walk to the canyon. There, he gives them a name and writes on smooth stones the way he was shown as a boy – *Tessa, Barney, Tish, Brodie, Pippa, Bear* – and places the stones face-down, exactly where they came from.

That's all Arlo knows. Uncle says he'll tell her more when it's her time.

Uncle and Heidi have been Arlo's foster parents since she was twelve; just over four years. She prefers not to remember who or what came before. She only knows that she belongs here, with the broken and unwanted. Here, they all have a purpose.

The chooks stir now, leaving their nests and squabbling at her feet. Arlo counts them. Twelve: six white, five brown, one black. Something squirms and nips at her right foot; she kicks her boot off and turns it upside-down, holds the torch between her teeth, shakes the boot. She doesn't look to see what bit her. They're too far from help anyway. Given time, most ailments go away on their own. She puts her boot back on, levers the lid from the feed bucket, and scatters three full scoops around the pen. The chooks know it's early: they're slow to leave the nest.

'Come on – chook, chook, chook.'

Her favourite, the black hen, stopped laying a week ago. Now she guards an empty nest and won't be shooed off, not by hands, feet or harsh words. Arlo slips her hand underneath hoping there might be an egg, but finds nothing.

The old hen pecks half-heartedly at her wrist, and Arlo feels like crying.

She collects nine eggs. After she has refilled the water trough in the yard and thrown the dogs' kibble, she heads back to the house.

Uncle sits on the hammocked couch on the porch, holding a steaming coffee cup in his good hand. Apart from his belly, the exact size and shape of a basketball under his shirt, he is hard lines and sharp angles, taut sinew and muscle. His thinning hair is wet at the collar.

'Morning,' she says, and waits. He takes a while to warm up to conversation.

'Black hen's not laying,' he says eventually.

'No, she did.' Arlo takes a still-warm egg from the apron pocket and shows him.

He doesn't believe her. 'She's scrawny. Give her to the dogs instead. Same difference in the end.'

Arlo unties the apron and hangs it on its hook with the eggs still cocooned inside. Unease cramps her belly. She's not supposed to get attached.

'Breakfast,' Heidi calls.

'Go eat. Deal with the hen straight after,' Uncle says, nodding at the door. 'It's her time.'

Arlo heads inside.

The kitchen is barely three by four metres: bench, oven, fridge, a four-seater table and a buffet hutch with mesh doors. She has to squeeze past Heidi, who's poaching eggs in a saucepan on the old stove, scooping spoonfuls of boiling water over the top. There'll be three for Uncle, two for herself, one for Arlo, a couple of pieces of toast each. It's the same every morning.

Heidi is still half-asleep, squinting, her blonde hair falling from a droopy bun on top of her head. 'You're not even dressed. Have you got time to eat? Don't want to miss the school bus.'

Arlo nods. 'I'll be quick.'

'You barely chew anyway.' Heidi goes to wash her hands in the laundry sink.

She has to make the decision, use her one chance now, otherwise Heidi will sit in the kitchen with her tea until Arlo leaves for the school bus and Uncle rides out on the quad or the tractor. She quietly opens the fridge and slips a packet of frozen bacon down the front of her pyjama bottoms.

When Heidi returns and Uncle takes his seat, she ignores the burning numbness starting at her navel. The toast is cold, the egg too hot. She mashes the egg and spreads it like paste, adds tomato sauce, makes a sandwich. It's not how she usually does it.

Heidi stares with her good eye. 'Don't forget your lunch.'

'Don't forget the hen,' Uncle adds.

Arlo eats half and holds the rest between her teeth while she rinses her plate. She doesn't have much time.

When she heads back out to the roost to deal with old hen, the dogs follow, sensing something is about to happen.

Arlo parks her creaky bike by the mailbox out on the road. The driveway leading to the house is over a kilometre long – she rides to the bus, otherwise her jeans get filthy and her shoes fill with dust. She has switched her school bag for Heidi's oversized backpack because she needs the extra room.

She shrugs off her jacket and leaves it hanging on the handlebars. It's chilly, but soon the heat will kick in. The school bus is coming over the rise, five minutes early. She steps out onto the road and lunges for the open door before the bus chugs to a complete stop.

'Hey,' she says to the driver.

'You're in a hurry.' Frank glances at her backpack, slowly checks her over. 'You running away from home?'

She detests him. He flicks his tongue like a lizard. He doesn't look girls in the eye, but in the chest.

'I'm not going anywhere you ain't taking me.' She wishes she'd kept her jacket on.

'Sit yourself down,' Frank says.

The Linney place is the third pick-up after the Aistropes and the Obsts, but with eight kids between the first two families, the bus is already half full.

Arlo hoped for a spot in the corner at the back, but settles for one midway. She sits, pushing the backpack under the seat in front, and the worst thing happens: Katie Obst moves next to her. Katie is sixteen too, but she's years behind in her head. About ten, Arlo thinks. Seven on a bad day. Her hair is in pigtails and she wears glitter shoelaces in her sneakers. Sometimes she comes looking for Arlo at the house and she has to walk her the three kilometres home. Katie's hands are always moving: pulling her hair, tugging her earlobes, plucking invisible strings and tapping invisible keys, as if she's trying to communicate using her own form of sign language.

'Go up the back, Katie,' she whispers. 'Go on, now.'

'Why?'

'I'm busy.'

'But why?' She winds a stray hair around her finger and yanks it out.

'I've got an assignment,' Arlo lies. 'I need some thinking time.' She puts her hand on the backpack. Katie turns, nudging it with her foot, and Arlo holds her breath. 'Go *on*.'

Katie starts crying.

'What'd you do to her?'

Arlo groans and shrinks in her seat. Cameron Obst only ever sticks up for his sister when it gives him an excuse to start something, and it looks like he's in a mood today.

'*Nothing*.' She smiles at Katie. 'Please – I'll take you to the canteen at lunch today. Okay?'

'Okay,' Katie says. She moves back to her seat.

But Cameron isn't letting it go. He shifts his hulking body into the space his sister left. Arlo can smell him: engine oil and stale sweat. He got a maroon Commodore wagon for his seventeenth birthday – she doesn't know why he can't just drive his brothers and sisters to school and free up some seats for the rest of them. She wants to tell him to where to go, but she doesn't need a scene.

'What up, freak,' he says.

'I didn't do anything.' She stares out the window at the wheat fields rushing past.

'Then why's she crying?'

'She's not now. She's fine.'

He splays his legs; his knee brushes hers. He calls her all the names, always the first to point out the map of tight scars puckering the left side of Arlo's body from neck to knee.

'Reckon your mother tried to boil you when you were a baby but you wouldn't fit in the pot.'

She tries not to wrinkle her nose at his sour breath. 'I don't remember how it happened,' she says, and it's the truth.

Uncle and Heidi don't know either, or if they do they've never told her. Never mention it, unless you count the one time Uncle said they were a fine trio, what with his three missing fingers and Heidi's sightless milky-blue eye.

Now the bus is stopping. Damon Uley gets on.

Cameron moves to another seat and says loudly, 'Hey, Damo – Linney's up for it but I'm not that desperate. Do you want to take out the trash?'

Damon mimes retching until his face turns purple.

Frank yells at him to either sit the hell down or get the hell off. Chaos ensues until the bus hits a hundred clicks.

Arlo takes the opportunity to check if the old black hen is still breathing.

She'd hypnotised her by stroking her belly and placed her gently on her back in the bottom of the bag. The dogs had gone bonkers for the bacon. The plan is to get off a stop early and set her free amongst Mrs Garrett's free rangers – she's too old and short-sighted to notice one more.

She slips her hand inside the bag and strokes the hen's neck feathers. She's awake and terrified, and it's another half hour to school at least. If Frank finds out he'll wring the chook's neck, or chuck her off in the middle of nowhere. If Uncle finds out he might decide Arlo doesn't belong after all – with Uncle you don't get many chances. He takes the ones nobody wants, but Arlo knows you can send foster kids back whenever you like, even after four years.

Katie again. 'I need to tell you something,' she says. *Tap, tap, tap.*

'Not *now*, Katie.'

The hen is sitting quietly but her heart is racing. Arlo is worried she'll go into shock. She closes the bag.

'I came to your house last night.'

'What? You can't do that! It's far and it's dangerous.' Arlo shakes her head. One day Katie won't make it home and she's willing to bet it's days before anyone notices she's missing. 'Something could've happened to you.'

Arlo is distracted by sound of the engine. They're fast approaching the intersection where Kel and Logan Murphy get on, but the bus isn't easing up. It's just like Kel to be late and Frank won't wait. She checks her watch. They're running about seven minutes early now.

'Don't forget the Murphys!' She sees two distant figures cutting through the line of trees in the front paddock, but Frank accelerates through the intersection. 'Frank! *Frank!*'

'Too late,' Frank says over his shoulder. 'You know the rule. If they ain't waiting, I ain't stopping.'

'Shit.' She punches the headrest in front and slumps back.

No amount of whining will get Frank to turn back – if anything, he's likely to shoot past the Linneys' the next time out of spite and Arlo hasn't missed the bus in years. It's a game to him.

'*Shit.*'

Katie leans forward. 'Arlo.'

'Katie, I said not *now*.'

Cameron's breath hits her. 'Stop messing with my sister, *freak*.'

Katie presses closer and looks at Arlo for reassurance. She

cowers when Damon Uley jumps into the seat behind them; he leans over, puts two fingers down his throat and makes gagging sounds. And before Arlo can react, Cameron reaches between her legs, grabs the backpack, and heaves it into the air where it begins a slow motion freefall. There's a sickening thud as he drop kicks it along the aisle.

Frank hits the brakes.

This time, Arlo can't hide her revulsion. She tells Cameron Obst where to go and he does. He takes Katie with him, drawing a line across his throat with his finger. She turns to watch him steer his sister along the aisle, with the other Obst kids hanging out the windows and Frank yelling at them to sit.

By the time she reaches into the backpack, she can already tell the hen's tiny heart has stopped.

Arlo carries the dead chicken around all day. It must be some kind of bad hoodoo: nothing goes right. She gets a C⁻ for her Chem test when she thought she did okay. Kel doesn't come to school, not even late, which leaves Arlo feeling raw like a skinned knee, and when she goes to her locker at lunchtime she realises she left her sandwiches behind on the kitchen table. To top it all off, Damon Uley lands a glob of spit on her back as she's closing the locker door.

In the girls' toilets, she contorts herself trying to wipe the spit away.

Arlo can't wait to leave this place. She has no secret dreams or big ambitions when her schooling is done. She only wants to stop looking over her shoulder, to not climb aboard the fetid bus each day, to be far from the schoolyard and its vicious politics. She will take care of the animals and wander the vast and mysterious landscape of the Linney acreage – thousands of acres, as yet undiscovered. Might even backpack around Australia, like Heidi did before she came to a stop here.

Arlo has heard the rumours: that Heidi never leaves the farm because she's not allowed, that Uncle kidnapped her, that he's a psychopath. But what she knows in her heart is simpler – something unspeakable happened to Heidi out there and Uncle saved her. Four years ago Uncle and Heidi saved her, too.

She remembers the chicken and feels sickening guilt. She can't risk being sent back. If Uncle asks for the truth, she'll give it.

She decides the spit is watered down enough not to pose a biological threat. Remembering her promise, she looks for Katie, shuffling past groups, suffering the usual stares and hissed insults –

> *freak*
> *Linney trash*
> *scab*
> *onion skin*
> *Frankenstein*

– knowing she makes it harder for herself because she never answers back. Silence upsets people. It's so much worse when Kel isn't here. The Murphys are untouchable; the name goes way back. But Heidi always says dignity is the greatest insult, so that's how Arlo plays it: head up, chin out, chewed tongue, and fists clenched to keep them from swinging.

Katie isn't waiting in her usual spot near the canteen. She won't line up by herself even if she has money to spend – other kids pressure her into buying things for them, or she gets confused trying to decide what she wants.

Arlo checks every spot Katie could be, leaving the most likely place for last. She has heard those rumours too, and it's not her business to intervene, but she finds herself heading for the maintenance shed because today she feels different. She can't put her finger on it – a faint call on the wind, a singing in her blood. An invisible thread reeling her in.

Behind the shed, Damon Uley and a group of older boys huddle together. Damon is collecting money, giving change. Cameron Obst is sitting on an upturned milk crate, holding court. And Katie Obst stands apart, her body hunched over and turned away, struggling to take off her bra without removing her T-shirt.

So this rumour was true: the boys paid Cameron to look at his sister's breasts.

The thread pulls tighter. Her blood hums.

She unzips the backpack. She grabs the hen's feet, brings her out and lifts her up, upside down and limp. She steps around the corner of the shed, widens her stance and raises the chicken like a weapon.

'Katie, let's go.'

A few of the guys mutter and step back.

Katie whimpers and covers her face.

Damon Uley says, 'Jesus. Is that thing dead?'

Arlo braces for retaliation, only she doesn't yet know what shape it will take.

Cameron rushes forward and catches her wrist. He drags her, feet scrabbling in the dirt, and Arlo drops the chicken. He flips her across his knee and raises her skirt. Somehow he has a stick in his hand. He whips her, hard, across the back of her thighs – once, twice, three times – and shoves her away so hard, she falls on her side in the dirt.

The bell goes.

Arlo slowly gets to her feet. She picks up her chicken.

Cameron laughs, head thrown back, his throat so dark and deep that Arlo thinks she can see hell inside.

After school Arlo sits at the front of the bus, right behind Frank. She's having trouble hearing and seeing: all noise from the back comes at her like she's underwater, and the view through the windscreen is blurred at the edges like a faded postcard.

She hopes this is what rage feels like, otherwise she fears she has given up.

When Frank overshoots the Linney driveway by a hundred metres, she doesn't mention it, doesn't complain, just gathers her things – bag, shoes, dead chicken – and steps off. She makes it the full distance before realising Katie got off the bus with her.

'Katie, what the hell?'

Katie mooches about near the letterbox, drawing circles in the dust with the toe of one glittery sneaker.

'Now how are you going to get home?'

'I'll walk.'

'I'm busy. There's something I have to do.'

'I'll help you.'

Arlo stares at the shimmering haze of exhaust left by the disappearing bus. She presents the handlebars of her bike for a dinky. 'Fine, but if you cry again I'm taking you home.'

'What are we doing?'

'We're going up the canyon.'

She always says that. They all do – they say up when really the canyon is down, a deep crack in the side of a perfectly rounded hill, as if the earth got too full and split open. Arlo has seen it from the top, but she has never been to the bottom.

She knows she screwed up. She has to make things right.

They skirt around the house. Arlo hides the bike in the hay shed. A couple of the dogs join them and they form a convoy: the girl with scars, a three-legged kelpie, a one-eared heeler, and the girl with the mind of a child. They follow the well-worn track, just wide enough for Uncle's tractor, as they make their way single-file past the creek, through the narrowest part of a shallow gorge, and up again along the camel-hump hills. The canyon begins where the side of the last hill falls away.

Arlo discards the backpack before descending. She cradles the chicken with one arm, using the other to steady herself, pressing her palm flat against the sheer rock face. The opposite side drops even more sharply, to a river of stones below. Uncle says no one knows where the water comes from or where it goes; it seems to trickle from a place inside the hill and disappear into the ground.

Today it's bone dry.

'It's dark,' Katie says when they reach the bottom. She points. 'What are they?'

Uncle brought a horse up last week. *Clyde, broken leg.* His skeleton is already picked clean, the bones scattered. The ribs remain upright like giant wishbones.

'They're the animals.'

Stillness all around and a hush, like waiting. Arlo wonders if it's always like this in the canyon, as if time has stopped and the rest of the world does not exist.

She lays the chicken gently on a large granite slab and strokes her head one last time. She chooses an egg-shaped stone and takes a marker from her pocket. She gives the chicken a name to take with her. This is all she knows.

'Can I tell you now?' Katie says, tugging at her earlobes.

'Tell me what?' Arlo is distracted. She thinks they probably shouldn't be speaking. 'Shhh.'

Conscious of the thread, pulling, and a faint vibration in her inner ear, she runs her hands lightly over the stones. One of them is singing to her. But which one?

'Cam says—'

Arlo looks up. 'Cam says what?'

Katie's eyes are glazed with fear. Her hands flutter, pulling at the ends of her hair. 'Cam says one day you'll disappear, just like the other foster kids. Then what will I do?'

Arlo's hand touches a stone roughly the size and shape of a human heart, and in that moment she understands what happens here in the canyon.

Sacrifice.

She picks up the stone, weighs it in her palms, turns the stone over, writes slowly, carefully, and places it back exactly where it came from.

The singing stops.

By the time she has walked Katie home and made it back to the house, the sun has set and Arlo is exhausted. Uncle is sitting on the porch, just the tip of his cigarette glowing as he draws back. Arlo freezes with one foot on the bottom step and, as expected, waits.

'You've been up the canyon,' he says eventually.

She knows better than to lie. 'Yeah. I did.'

'Thought I told you to give the chook to the dogs.'

'I took her,' she confesses. 'I wanted to save her but she died anyway.'

Uncle shakes his head. 'It was her time. Nothing you did would've changed that. What else?'

'I *felt* it. I know everything,' she says quietly. 'Or I think I do.'

His eyes glint in the dark. 'Then you know you can't leave.'

She tells the truth. 'I never wanted to.'

Uncle stands, beckons her close, and rests his heavy, fingerless hand on her shoulder. When she was younger, Arlo would flinch if he touched her with that stump. An accident with an axe, a moment of carelessness, a knife fight – Uncle tells a different story every time, says it doesn't matter how he lost them because Heidi was worth every finger.

'Can't ask for more than you're owed, child,' he says.

Arlo finds she is shaking. Her blood is sluggish and cold. 'What if I asked for someone else?'

'You'll know by morning.'

Countless times Arlo has prayed for sleep when it seemed out of reach, but never before has she wished she could stay awake.

At ten o'clock a northerly whips up, buffeting the house, carrying dirt and leaves and anything not tied down. Arlo watches as an inch of red dust builds on the ledge outside her bedroom window. When she's sure Uncle and Heidi are asleep she sneaks out onto the porch, calls out quietly, snaps her fingers. The dogs emerge like slinking shadows to follow her inside – boss dog first – heads down, long nails clicking on the floorboards. One by one they jump onto the bed, turning circles and curling into her hollows.

The phone rings at midnight; shortly after, she hears Uncle moving around, shrugging into his Emergency Services gear, driving away in the ute. There'll be trees down, maybe power lines.

By two she has finished reading almost an entire novel and Uncle hasn't returned. Her eyes ache. Her body is heavy, as if she has weights attached to her wrists and ankles. The dogs are jumpy, alert to every sound.

When she does sleep, it's the kind that feels like falling.

Morning. Uncle is sitting at the table, shoulders slumped with exhaustion, still wearing his hi-vis jacket. Heidi has made toast and a pot of tea.

Arlo's fault – she has slept so late she hasn't collected the eggs. She lingers in the hall, listening.

'You were out a long time,' Heidi says. 'Trees down?'

Uncle sighs. 'Obst kid. The eldest. Rolled his car on the big bend.'

'Drinking?'

'Heart, I heard.'

Heidi chokes on her tea. 'How bad?'

In the silence before Uncle can reply, Arlo's breath hisses between her teeth. Her legs buckle. She sees herself writing on the stone, Cameron's red throat, the car rolling, twisted metal.

'He'll live,' Uncle says.

Heidi spots her. She squints her good eye, as if she can see better with the blind one.

'Come on in here.' Uncle turns his head slowly as Arlo enters.

His gaze sweeps her body as if he's taking inventory. 'Obst boy's in hospital. You know anything about that?'

Dumbly, she shakes her head.

'Might be a hard day at school today.'

Arlo nods. If she tries to speak, her insides will come up.

'Stay home if you want. Heidi could use the help.'

She nods again.

'Cat got your tongue?' he asks.

In an instant he has reached up and squeezed her cheeks, forcing Arlo to open her mouth. Her tongue rolls out like a carpet. Arlo steps back, shocked, and Uncle and Heidi give relieved laughs in unison.

'I'm going to school. Might be a good day today.'

Heidi turns to the sink as if for support. Her shoulders are shaking.

'Sit down, Arlo,' Uncle says.

She sits.

'Tell us what you know.'

She tries to explain. 'I *felt* it. What is it? Is it a *thing*?'

Uncle looks at Heidi. 'We've never seen it. It's old. We feed it and it stays where it is. Sometimes if you ask it will give, but if you ask too much it takes.' He rubs his face. 'It goes back generations – Heidi and I chose to never have kids, so I thought this was the end of it. I was the last one.'

'It brought you here,' Heidi says suddenly. 'We didn't choose you. *It* did. Another year and you would have been grown up and gone. Now you're its caretaker. Why didn't you just stay away?'

'I couldn't,' Arlo says. 'It sang to me.'

Arlo shoos the lazy dogs from her room.

She dresses for school, does a quick job of brushing her hair and teeth. The tiredness and shock are fading and she thinks she might float off, carried by an unnamed emotion that makes her light as air.

As she rides to the letterbox, every muscle sparks with electricity. There is no wind; the sky is endlessly clear and blue.

When she reaches the gate, Arlo dismounts to find she is unsteady on her feet. She drops her bag and staggers sideways, clutching at the gate to right herself. A damned stone in her shoe – but here is the bus, early as usual.

Frank opens the door. Arlo doesn't acknowledge him. She strides along the aisle, heading for the back seat. It's the usual crowd, minus one. They scatter, all except Katie, and Arlo sits where she wants.

'What you did—' Katie says, staring straight ahead. 'I'm not stupid.'

'Never said you were.'

'I can *read*.'

'Katie, you don't have to do anything those boys tell you to do again, not ever.'

She takes Katie's hands and they are finally still – no endless plucking and pulling. Arlo notices how beautiful her grey eyes are, how clear and perfect her skin. Her expression is serene. She is damaged but not broken, and Arlo plans to keep it that way.

The bus shoots past the Uley stop. No Damon. This day just keeps getting better. Ten minutes later they're approaching the intersection where Kel and Logan get on.

Arlo squeezes past Katie, slides out of her seat, and sits behind Frank.

'Don't forget the Murphys.'

Kel and Logan are already climbing the last fence. They're easily on time, but Frank doesn't take his eyes from the road. He accelerates. His cheek is wrinkled like the skin on a tin of paint.

Arlo isn't smiling. She has had enough of the game.

She presses her lips to his ear. 'Stop the bus,' she whispers, and her voice is ancient, full of dirt.

Yeah, the Murphys go way back, but even Frank knows the Linney name goes further back than anyone can remember.

He brakes and pulls over.

When the bus arrives at school and everyone else gets off, Arlo can no longer ignore the pinch in her right boot. She kicks off the boot and turns it upside-down, shakes it. She lifts her leg to peel her sock away from her foot.

Not a stone. Not something that is there. Something that is not.

Her smallest toe is gone – no evidence of a cut or bleeding, but sheared away smoothly without leaving a scar.

It must have happened some time in the night. She should have known when Uncle told Heidi: *He'll live.*

It wasn't quite what she'd asked for.

Stop Revive Survive

SARAH EPSTEIN

Eddie's bladder was going to burst. It was all he could think about. He readjusted himself in the passenger seat, loosening the seatbelt across his lap. Every bump and dip in the road sent stabbing pains through his abdomen.

'Pull over here,' he begged his cousin Stu, regretting the large Coke he'd ordered with his burger and fries at their last stop. 'The emergency lane will do.'

'Nup,' Stu said. 'Too dangerous.'

Eddie stared through the windscreen at the two northbound lanes of rural highway. A metal guardrail ran the length of the shoulder, but there was ample room for a car to pull over.

'How's it dangerous?' Eddie asked. 'There are barely any cars around.'

Stu checked his mirrors, squinting at the burnt-orange sunset behind them. 'Haven't you ever watched dash-cam videos? Cars in highway emergency lanes get smashed into all the time. Only takes one distracted driver and *bam*.'

He took both hands off the wheel for a second, slapping his palms together like he was squashing a bug. He was talking crap as usual; Eddie knew Stu was just doing this to torture him. His cousin had always been a bit of a dick, and things had intensified since Stu finished high school and started a traineeship at a marketing company. As far as Eddie could tell, Stu's co-workers were absolute tools, always bragging about women and cars and how much money they made. And they referred to themselves as the 'Alpha Pack'. Enough said.

'Just pull over anywhere!'

Eddie started to sweat. He was even eyeing up the empty Coke cup in the cup holder and hoped it wouldn't come to that. If he pissed himself in Aunty Meg's car, not only would she be furious with him, but Stu would never let him live it down.

'There,' his cousin said, pointing out a blue road sign ahead. It showed a symbol of a tree with a picnic table – *5 km* – and three words stacked, one on top of the other:

STOP

REVIVE

SURVIVE.

'Good timing,' Stu added. 'I need a break.'

Never mind that I needed one twenty minutes ago, Eddie thought, rolling his eyes.

This road trip had been his mother's idea, but Eddie couldn't hold it against her. In fact, there wasn't any other way around it if he wanted to make it to Sydney in time to see his grandfather on his deathbed. *A mercy dash*, Eddie's mum called it. Grandpa Mac had taken a turn for the worse yesterday and nursing staff advised he was nearing the end. The nine-hour drive from Melbourne to Sydney would still be faster than the rigmarole of booking expensive last-minute flights, not to mention all the waiting around for transfers in between. Eddie's mum and Aunty Meg flew to Sydney a week ago, and they suggested Stu drive up there in his mother's car with Eddie. Only problem with the whole plan was that Eddie would be stuck in an enclosed space with Stu for the best part of a day. And ten minutes into the drive, he realised he'd made a huge mistake.

That was seven hours ago.

Stu yawned. 'Oh man, I'm so shattered,' he said, rubbing a hand over his face. 'Big one with the boys last night. Should've seen the girls all over us at the club. They can't resist the alpha energy.'

Eddie gritted his teeth and turned towards the passenger window. It was the same view he'd been looking at for hours: brown grass, scrubby trees, jagged rock cuttings, wire fences stretching on forever. He rested his head against the glass and closed his eyes, wishing he could put his earbuds in to drown Stu out. His phone was low on battery though, and he needed it to keep his mum updated. Mercifully, it wasn't long until the tick of the car's indicator made Eddie sit up. Stu merged into the turning lane for the rest stop. *Thank god.*

As they pulled off the Hume Highway, the sealed surface gave way to a gravel side-road. It meandered a short distance before curving around a picnic ground surrounded by tall eucalypts. The other side of the rest area backed onto a forest, dense pine trees rolling out as far as the eye could see. Three sad-looking wooden picnic tables sat empty, and the grass was an overgrown haven for snakes and who knew what else. It hadn't been maintained for a while by the look of things, which didn't bode well for the state of the toilets.

'Bummer,' Stu said, bumping the car through the potholed parking area. 'I was hoping it would be one of those driver revivers with free coffee and biscuits.'

The place was deserted, except for a motorhome parked at the far end with its cabin door open. Two empty fold-up chairs were positioned in front of it, one tipped on its side.

'They probably only run them during school holidays,' Eddie said, distracted. He'd spotted the toilet block through the trees. It was about fifty metres from the parking area towards the edge of the pine forest. He already had his seatbelt unbuckled and fingers gripped around the door handle.

The moment the car stopped, Eddie scrambled up the narrow dirt trail towards the toilets. They were in a tiny dark green building with a corrugated roof. A water tank sat nearby with a tap on the side and a plastic sign reading *Non-potable – Do Not Drink*. Eddie guessed the toilets were long drops before he even made it near the door. The air was rancid. The kind of stink that soured in your mouth and shrivelled your windpipe all the way to your lungs.

Eddie decided to bypass that horror show altogether. He slipped into the trees at the edge of the forest, letting out a shuddering sigh as he relieved himself onto a carpet of dead pine needles. He glanced over his shoulder to make sure he couldn't be seen from the motorhome. All quiet over there. Feeling himself relax as he emptied out, Eddie let his eyes roam up the long corridors of trees. The air smelled spicy and refreshing, like his family's living room at Christmas-time. One nearby pine even had a scrap of red and white polka-dot fabric snagged in a lower branch, flapping in the breeze like a festive flag. Eddie peered up further into the canopy and noticed a number of broken boughs, splintered from their trunks and dangling.

As Eddie zipped up his fly, a car door thumped closed in the distance. He glanced over at Aunty Meg's sedan to see Stu moving to one of the rear doors.

What the hell's he up to?

Something snapped in the forest. Eddie spun around and stared into the trees. The light was fading now, long shadows merging in the blue-grey dusk. Eddie held still, scouring for movement between the long rows of tree trunks. Probably just an animal – a roo or a wombat – and hopefully not some weirdo from the motorhome spying on him while he peed.

Only now did Eddie realise he couldn't hear any wildlife. No birds or crickets. Not even a fly buzzing past. Just the subtle creak of swaying pines, a hiss of wind, and the occasional distant *whoosh* of passing vehicles out on the highway.

On his return to the car, Eddie paused at the water tank to wash his hands. He heard a much louder crack in the forest this time, like a tree branch splitting in half. Something heavy thumped to the ground. Campers collecting firewood? Maybe. Eddie wasn't sticking around to find out. He felt exposed out here in the open, even more so scurrying back to the car park with the forest behind him.

He found Stu sprawled across the sedan's rear seat, his limbs bent at awkward angles. One arm was raised alongside his head, folded at the elbow and draped across his eyes.

'What are you doing?' Eddie asked.

'Power nap.'

Eddie glanced at the forest as he pulled the passenger door shut behind him. 'We should keep moving. It's getting dark.'

'Exactly. So I need to be alert,' Stu said. He shifted to get comfortable. 'When you actually know how to drive, you'll understand.'

Eddie ignored the dig. Stu always spoke to him like he was six instead of sixteen. 'You know this is that area though, right?'

'Which area?'

'Where those backpackers disappeared.'

'What, like thirty years ago?' Stu's tone was mocking. He didn't bother lifting his arm to look at Eddie. 'The dude who killed them went to prison and died of cancer. I think we'll be okay.'

'I don't mean that,' Eddie said. 'It happened earlier this year. A couple of Dutch tourists disappeared along this stretch.'

'So?'

'Their backpacks were found on the side of the highway. Police suspect foul play.' Stu didn't respond, so Eddie continued. 'Another hitch-hiker came forward saying he'd been picked up by some guy who had all this dodgy stuff in his car. Ropes, duct tape, a handsaw—'

Stu yawned. 'You're getting it confused with a movie.'

'I can google it right now if you don't believe me.'

'Jesus, Ed.' Stu shifted again. 'I just need twenty minutes. Keep the bloody doors locked if you're so scared.'

'I'm just saying—' Eddie stopped and sighed. Of course Stu didn't believe him. His cousin was one of those people who always had to be right, and if it turned out anyone else was, he feigned disinterest or changed the subject.

'Better make it thirty minutes,' Stu mumbled.

It'll be pitch black by then, Eddie didn't say out loud. He waited until Stu's breathing slowed, then leaned over the driver's seat to hit the central-locking button on the car keys. They weren't in the ignition though. In Stu's pocket most likely. Eddie flicked the door lock on the driver's side and a satisfying clunk locked all four doors simultaneously.

Minutes passed. The car's engine ticked. The wind picked up a little, just enough to scatter dead leaves across the car park. Eddie slid a curious glance towards the motorhome. Where were the owners? There was a large patch of disturbed gravel between the fold-up chairs and the cabin door. A small object sat abandoned on the step inside the cabin. A sandal. Just one.

Crack!

Whump.

Eddie jerked in his seat, swinging back towards the passenger window. Something in the pine forest had splintered and dropped. It was big. Loud enough to hear from inside the car. Eddie pressed his nose to the glass and held his breath. He watched the silhouetted treetops, now almost black against the hazy evening sky.

A tree shook.

Then the one beside it.

Eddie squinted, struggling to focus in the dwindling light. Another pine tree swayed, the top half rocking like a pendulum. It was as if something was moving from tree to tree.

Something large.

Nah. It had to be the wind. Or a flock of birds.

You haven't heard a single bird call, Eddie reminded himself.

But what kind of animal could it possibly be?

Eddie couldn't help it: his mind started running through ridiculous possibilities. Yowie, Sasquatch, Bigfoot – every other folklore creature he could think of that didn't really exist. Hell, maybe they did. What did Eddie know? His dying grandfather certainly believed in that sort of stuff. A grizzled Scotsman who grew up in Inverness, Grandpa Mac used to show Eddie and Stu a blurry Polaroid he took of a dark splotch in the water he claimed was the head of the Loch Ness Monster. 'The thing about monsters,' he'd say with a wink, 'is they appear when ye least expect 'em. So ye have to be ready, ye ken?'

Eddie groped around inside the car's console. He shoved his hand down the side of the seat, then along the floor at his feet. He popped open the glovebox. Beneath a packet of wet wipes and the car owner's manual, his fingers closed around a steel wrench. It felt weighty, reassuring. He turned his attention to the forest again and held his breath. Nothing moved now. The wind had died down and the trees were still. So still that Eddie questioned whether they'd really moved at all.

Quiet descended on the rest area. Stu's breathing was rhythmic and lulling. Eddie felt his shoulders relax, his grip loosening on the wrench. He could hear crickets now as the last remnants of orange leached from the sky. Slumping against the seat, Eddie stretched his legs out and felt the tension in his limbs dissolving as he—

'Aah-aaa-aah-aaaah-aaa-aah-aaaah-aah . . . Thun-der!'

Eddie startled, whacking the wrench into his kneecap. Stu's ringtone cut through the silence, the opening bars of AC/DC's 'Thunderstruck'.

His cousin jolted upright. He blinked into the grey light, disorientated, before pulling out his phone. Eddie quickly shoved the wrench into the pocket of his cargo pants before Stu could see it.

'Mum?' Stu answered. He wiped the drool from the corner of his mouth. Eddie heard the squawk of Aunty Meg's voice on the other end but couldn't catch what she was saying. Stu didn't look alarmed; it couldn't have been the inevitable news about their grandpa just yet.

'No worries,' Stu said, stifling a yawn. 'Just taking a quick break. We'll be back on the road in five.' He hung up, stretched his neck muscles, then tried to open the car door and found it locked. He shook his head at Eddie. 'Wuss,' he muttered, reaching for the keys in his pocket.

Eddie clambered out of the car after him. 'What'd your mum say?'

Stu ignored him as he moved to the driver's door. 'I'm thirsty as hell,' he said, reaching inside for his water bottle. He gave it a shake but it was empty. 'There's a tap up there at the toilets, right?'

'A sign says *Do Not Drink*.'

'Damn.' Stu glanced over his shoulder at the motorhome. 'Go and ask them if they can spare some.' He tossed the plastic bottle at Eddie, who fumbled to catch it.

'What? Why me?'

Stu headed for the dirt trail. 'Because I've been driving all day, Ed. It's the least you can do.'

'Wait.' Eddie looked past Stu towards the pine trees. 'Where are you going?'

'What does it look like? You wanna come and hold my hand?'

'Just go here,' Eddie said. 'Behind the car.' His tone was childish, even to his own ears. He quickly added, 'The long drop stinks like somebody died in there.'

'Don't have a choice, mate,' Stu called, jogging up the trail. 'Not keen on crapping in the car park.'

Eddie studied the forest for a moment, then reluctantly turned and trudged across the parking area towards the motorhome. The grey gloom of evening had set in, but there were no lights on inside.

'Hello?' he called. His eyes were drawn to that single sandal again, a long smear of mud beside it on the step. 'Anybody home?' He glanced over his shoulder in time to see Stu disappear inside the toilets. They'd be on the road again soon enough.

A few metres from the motorhome, it hit Eddie: an odour ten times worse than the long drop. Spoiled meat and bin juice and sewage all rolled into one. He slapped a hand across his mouth and stumbled backwards for fresh air, taking a few bracing gulps before reaching for his phone. He flicked on the light and shone it towards the motorhome's door.

The smear of mud on the doorstep was reddish-brown and glistening. Droplets of it were spattered up the internal walls.

Oh god.

Long streaks of it marked the laminate floor like something had been dragged.

It wasn't mud at all.

'Stu!' Eddie yelled, whirling around. 'STU!'

His frantic voice echoed across the rest area. Stu had mocked him about the serial killer stuff, but this looked bad. Really, really bad.

'Stu!' he called again. He was frozen with indecision. Return to the car? Or check if someone inside the motorhome needed help?

Does it smell like they can be helped?

Stu emerged from the toilets. In the dim light, Eddie could make him out, hastily buttoning his jeans.

'*What the hell!*' Stu shouted, stumbling on the trail. His phone's torch blinked on, directed at his feet. His gait was stroppy, clearly irritated. '*You can't be alone for two minutes, you friggen' baby!*'

Behind him, movement rippled through the trees.

One by one, the pines shook, as if in sequence. Stu turned at the sound of splitting branches. A large shadow thrashed closer and closer to the forest's edge until—

It burst out of the treetops.

'What the fu—' Eddie gasped.

A hulking creature arced through the air and thudded to the ground beside the toilet block. Four-legged and front-heavy, five times the size of Stu. Skin black as night and a bulbous head like a tumour, split sideways to reveal a gaping maw for a mouth.

What am I looking at? Eddie's brain shrieked. *Whatthehellis thatthing!*

He didn't realise he was backing away until he smacked into the motorhome's siding.

The creature hunched forward on hooked limbs, angling its head one way, then the other.

Stu ran. He sprinted down the dirt trail so fast, his phone sailed out of his hand, the torch light spinning to the ground. The creature launched itself after him, bounding on all fours like an oversized attack dog, kicking up grass and soil in its wake. The gap between them closed quickly. Stu yelped as he vaulted over the car park's log edging, fumbling for the keys in his pocket as he rounded the car. The creature leapt too, its bulk making it less agile. It skidded right past the vehicle across the gravel.

To Eddie's horror, it was headed straight for him.

He bolted up the motorhome's steps and yanked the door shut, ducking low behind the kitchenette to brace for impact. The creature slammed into the side of the van, so hard it rocked from side to side. Plastic cups and plates rained down over Eddie as he gulped for air in the thick stench. His phone light bounced off the ceiling, illuminating the back half of the cabin.

A cry caught in his throat.

Slumped face-down on the floor was the body of a woman, her red and white polka-dot dress in tatters.

Her left ankle was a meaty mess. Her right leg had been torn off mid-thigh. And blood. So much blood. It pooled beneath her like a black hole in the laminate flooring.

Eddie pressed his eyes shut, woozy. He panted so fast he might faint.

Outside, Aunty Meg's car started up.

Wait.

Eddie lurched towards the closest window. The creature was on the other side of the glass. Eddie froze, didn't blink. He held his breath and watched the creature's head tilt towards the engine noise. Up close its skin was leathery and toad-like, rippling just beneath the surface like a carcass full of maggots. It had sunken voids where its eyes should be. A bumpy spine protruded down the full length of its back.

The creature opened its mouth, baring several rows of jagged teeth. It made a throaty clicking sound, insect-like and alien.

Across the car park, Stu gunned the sedan's engine, wheels spinning wildly in the gravel. He floored it towards the exit, his horrified face peering through the driver's window long enough to make eye contact with Eddie.

'Wait!' Eddie shouted, slamming a hand against the motorhome's window. The creature jerked back to the glass for a heart-stopping second before taking off after the car.

Eddie threw open the motorhome's door and tumbled out, waving his arms. 'Stu! Wait!'

He'll turn around. He'll come back to get me.

The sedan skidded onto the side road towards the highway, the engine kicking up a notch. Not slowing. Not doubling back.

'Don't leave me here!' Eddie cried.

As the car followed the curve of the side road, the creature cut through the picnic ground, using its limbs against gum trees to effortlessly propel itself forward. It met the vehicle at the other side of the long grass, leaping through the air and landing on the bonnet like a boulder. Eddie heard a crunch of metal. One of the tyres popped. The sedan spun out sideways as Stu lost control. It slammed into a tree and the creature was thrown off-balance. But only for a second. It reared up on its hind legs before thrusting its head through the windscreen.

Eddie couldn't move. His pulse thrashed in his ears as he watched the creature rummage, half-in, half-out of the car. Stu's screams of agony made Eddie's legs weak.

What do I do? What do I do?

As his cousin's cries dwindled into wet gurgles, a chill of terror washed over Eddie. He was next. He needed to run ... but where? He could see headlights on the highway, oblivious motorists going about their Thursday evening. If he made it out there he could flag down a car, get to safety, tell people. They'd come here and hunt it.

Destroy it.

But what about the creature's speed? It would snatch Eddie

up before he made it across the picnic ground. If he hid in the motorhome it was only a matter of time before the creature smashed those windows too. Eddie would bleed to death in there like the woman in the polka-dot dress. He didn't want to die on the side of a highway. He didn't want to die alone.

He didn't want to die.

Eddie dashed to the nearest gum tree. He slipped behind the wide trunk and listened for movement, daring a peek towards the sedan.

The creature was busy feeding. On Stu.

Eddie swallowed the bile rising in the back of his throat. He eyed up the next tree a few metres away. As he snuck towards it, the toe of his shoe caught on a tree root. He stumbled, scraping his foot loudly in the dirt. Eddie pressed himself flat against the tree and held his breath. Seconds passed like hours. He took another glimpse across the picnic ground.

Still feeding. Keep going.

Eddie dashed to the next tree. Then the next one. The edge of the picnic ground was in sight. But to run from the side road to the highway, Eddie needed to pass Aunty Meg's car. He edged around the tree for a better vantage point, gingerly navigating his feet between tree roots. He felt a twig crunch beneath his foot at the exact moment he heard a loud, dry *snap.*

The creature extracted itself from the car. It sprang from the bonnet and prowled the picnic ground, mouth slick with blood. Scraps of Stu's T-shirt and other things Eddie didn't want to think about were dangling from its teeth.

Eddie was stuck. He couldn't run for the highway. He couldn't make it back to the motorhome. The creature cocked its head, producing the clicking noise again. Eddie's blood ran cold. Was it listening for him? Tracking him? It responded to sound when Stu started the car. If something drew it away, Eddie could make a break for it.

Call for help.

Eddie carefully slid his phone from his pocket. The battery was almost dead but he might manage one call. How could he do it without the creature hearing him speak?

He could set an alarm, toss his phone somewhere to lure the creature away. But how far could he throw? To give himself a fighting chance it would need to be an impossible distance, all the way up near the forest's edge like—

Stu's phone.

Eddie looked beyond the picnic ground, past the motorhome to the other side of the car park. Halfway along the dirt trail was the faint glow of the phone's torch light.

He dialled Stu's number. The ringtone sang out in the darkness.

'Aah-aaa-aah-aaaah-aaa-aah-aaaah-aah . . . Thun-der!'

From here it wasn't loud, but the creature jerked upright, alert.

'Aah-aaa-aah-aaaah-aaa-aah-aaaah-aah . . . Thun-der!'

Twisting its hulking frame, it charged towards the sound.

Eddie bolted.

Long grass whipped at his cargo pants. Dry leaves crunched beneath his feet. His footfalls echoed when he hit the side road. *Too loud too loud too loud.* Eddie pressed the phone to his ear. As soon as it diverted to voicemail he hung up and redialled Stu's number with trembling hands. He couldn't look behind him. If he was going to be snatched up by that thing, he didn't want to see it coming.

The gravel turned to bitumen as Eddie hurtled onto the

highway. He dialled Stu's number again but his phone turned black and silent. Headlights blazed in the distance and Eddie sprinted towards them. There were no streetlights out here. Cars wouldn't see him until they were almost on top of him.

A ute with a chrome bull bar approached at speed. Eddie knew the driver had spotted him when the high beams flashed on and off.

He waved his arms above his head. 'Stop! Help!'

The driver blasted the horn and swerved, forcing Eddie backwards onto the shoulder.

'*Get off the road, meth-head!*' somebody yelled as the ute flew by.

Eddie winced. That car horn was way too loud. Any minute now, that thing would come bounding up the side road.

Chest burning, he pushed on further down the highway. A semi-trailer drew close, lit up like a Christmas tree. Eddie stayed on the shoulder this time, jumping up and down and swinging his arms wildly. The truck thundered past without even slowing.

Eddie choked back tears of frustration.

The next car *had* to stop. He'd throw himself across the bonnet if need be.

One more set of headlights glowed in the darkness.

Please please please.

Eddie waved his arms as he ran towards it. Miraculously, the car's indicator blinked as it pulled into the emergency lane. Eddie staggered to the passenger side and tried to open the door. It was locked. The driver lowered the window.

'Please,' Eddie gasped, doubling over. 'Please let me in.'

A man his dad's age was behind the wheel. Balding, with

glasses and a flannelette checked shirt. 'You look like you've had a rough night.'

'Please help me,' Eddie managed. He looked back towards the rest area. Was that movement on the side road? *Please. We were attacked.*'

The man recoiled.

'You need to get me out of here,' Eddie pleaded.

The driver hesitated for a moment before leaning over to unlock the door.

'Open it,' he said. 'Get in.'

Eddie collapsed into the passenger seat and slammed the door shut. 'Drive. You need to drive right now!'

The man gave him a quick once-over before checking his mirrors and pulling onto the highway. 'What the hell happened?'

Eddie tugged on his seatbelt. 'This animal, this creature. It—' He couldn't find words to describe it. 'It came out of nowhere.'

'What?' The driver nudged his glasses and gave Eddie a doubtful glance. 'I drive up and down this area all the time for work. I've never heard about any ferocious wild animals.'

'Trust me,' Eddie said, trying to force the memory of Stu's screams from his mind.

'Who are you with?' the driver asked. 'Does anyone know you're here?'

'My cousin . . . ' Eddie's voice broke. 'I was with my cousin. But this thing – it attacked him. And a woman too. She was already . . .'

Eddie shook his head, unable to look at the driver as he tried to hold himself together.

'You're safe now,' the driver said. A subtle change in his voice made Eddie look over. The dashboard lights were reflected in his glasses. 'We'll get you some help.'

Did he think Eddie was crazy? On drugs? Maybe he thought Eddie was lying.

'I need the police,' Eddie said.

'Do you have a phone?'

Eddie held it up with a shaky hand. 'Battery died.'

'My phone's in the back. You want me to pull over and get it?'

'No!' Eddie turned to look through the rear window. The black outline of the pine forest was still too close. 'Not yet. Please keep driving.'

The car hit a bump and rattled. Eddie's eyes were drawn to the junk spread across the back seat. A duffle bag. Rope. A roll of garbage bags.

A handsaw.

'Just relax now,' the driver said. 'I'll take care of you.'

Eddie glanced at the passenger door. The handle had been removed.

'Where are we going?' Eddie asked as the driver drifted into a turning lane. A rural backroad was coming up. No streetlights. Not signposted.

The driver flexed his fingers, then re-gripped the steering wheel.

'We need the police,' Eddie insisted. 'The army. *Something.*'

The driver was quiet, his attention on the road.

Eddie's heartrate had barely slowed before it surged again. He thought of Grandpa Mac, who he wanted to see one last time.

The thing about monsters is they appear when ye least expect 'em.

'So you have to be ready,' Eddie murmured.

He unbuckled his seatbelt and reached for the wrench in his pocket.

Don't Look!

LISA FULLER

I shove my face against the window frame, letting the breeze brush over me. Wishing it was cool. No relief is coming. Not even after the sun goes down. Mid-summer afternoons in our rural hometown are my worst nightmare. We only rolled into town an hour ago and I already want to escape.

Sweat dribbles into my eyes and I blink them open, staring out at the bleached brown land. Small puffs of air churn the dirt. The odd willy-willy stirs the dust and dead bark and leaves from shedding trees. I feel like I'm melting into my chair. My sweat soaking into the couch does nothing to soften its prickly texture.

Mum and the aunties sit around the kitchen table. Catching up on all the latest gossip. I don't know where they find the energy.

We haven't been home in almost a year, not since Nick. The platitudes from all the mob had finally stopped after I'd walked over here. If one more person told me he would 'always be with me', I'd scream. He wasn't with me. That was the fucking point.

'Whatchu lookin at?' My cousin Candy plonks down beside me, saving me from my own thoughts and rising tears. Somehow she looks fresh, not like a sweaty turd. We're the same age, but she's always seemed *more* than me. More intelligent, good-looking, kind, everything. Just more. I'd hate her if I didn't love her so much.

'Nuthin. Whatchu doin?' My accent shifts when I'm home. My attitude, my body language. Mob way, Mum says. Proper way, Dad adds.

'Gotta babysit the kids tonight, wanna come help?' I hesitate. Her little sister Katie turned eight last week and will be easy to care for, but their brother Tyrone is only just toddling. That means dirty nappies and the ability to run away and get into anything and everything.

'Who's watchin em now?' I look over at her mum, Aunty Trina, and I know Uncle Rick is out the back with the men.

'Grams got em, but Mum wants er ere to yarn too.' She shifts into sad-eyes mode. 'Please cuz, I don't wanna be alone. Mum promised me takeaway and that I can rent some movies. I'll let ya pick.'

'Fine, ya big con artist,' I chuckle.

With a grin that shows both her dimples, she winks. 'Good, we can catch up too.'

I grimace as she wiggles her eyebrows at me. My smart cuz just cannot fathom the desert that is my love life. To her mind, living in a big city means a bigger dating pool. If she fails to see my less attractive qualities, it's not like I want to point them out to her. Back here I was just one of the cousins. Not the weirdo with her tiny but tight-knit friend group. The one with the parents who guard her like rottweilers.

'Ya ready niece?' Uncle Warren calls from the back door.

Candy hops up, waving me to follow. 'Aunty, Raina's comin with me.'

Mum looks over and frowns. 'Where?'

'Babysittin the kids so you fullas can ave a drink.'

I hold my breath. Hoping to get some space at last. Mum looks to Aunty Trina, who's digging in her purse, before pulling out some notes and handing them to her daughter. 'Gorn then, but no goin out anywhere else.'

I roll my eyes, turning to hide my slow breath out. Candy just laughs again. 'Course not Aunty, we're good girls.'

The women at the table scoff as we pass on our way out the back. We walk through the men clustered in the shade of the old water tank, and Dad gives me a shout. Candy sweet-talks him and we climb into Uncle's old dual-cab. I notice a hunched figure sitting to the side, arms folded and glaring at everyone.

'What's with Gramps? How come e's not up with Grams?' You normally never saw the one without the other.

I can see Candy shrug. 'Some fight e ad with my mum and dad. He and Grams don't agree.'

Uncle Warren chuckled while he pulled out a rollie and lit up. 'It's that house, he never wanted you movin in there.'

'How come?' I leant forward so I could see the side of his face.

'Better ask im,' Uncle reverses, hitting play on his car stereo. Alan Jones croons about rocking jukeboxes as I stare out at the same copy-and-paste landscape. Paint-shedding weatherboards line the streets, alternating with patches of scrub. The wind coming through the window is slightly less hot.

I feel a lightness in my chest, knowing I've been allowed out. Being home has other benefits. Normally if I want any space, I'd have to sneak out. Resentment curdles in my guts at what they'd forced me to do. It's not like I was off drinking or doing drugs. Just hanging out in one of my girls' houses, giggling and carrying on. But they still tried to ban me. Mum and Dad don't understand, sometimes I need to forget. To be in a house that isn't filled to the ceiling with pain. Ever since Nick.

I let my head flop to the side, whacking the car door hard enough to rattle the thoughts away. Focusing on the song, I hum along to the lyrics. Uncle Warren sings them top-note.

Pulling up outside the local corner shop, we hop out while Uncle fills up his car. We order Golden Fried Chicken with loads of chips and gravy, then set to haggling over the movie. Candy doesn't let me pick, but I knew she wouldn't. I ban a few I've already seen and then leave her to it. Chocolates, ice cream and Tristram's Cherry Cheer round it out, filling our plastic bag to the brim. God I missed this.

Minutes later, we roll up to Aunty Trina and Uncle Rick's new place. It's a lot like their old house, just bigger, with different colours. Another weatherboard on small stumps with peeling cream paint and a faded green roof. A recently added wooden porch extends out the front.

Their old place had three bedrooms, but this one has five. Candy has filled me in on the new joys of sharing a room with just one other sister, not four. They have ten kids total, but most of them have taken off to various family places for the school holidays. Candy is the eldest, and she only stayed because of her new boyfriend, she whispered to me. Only the two youngest ones are still at home. From the car we can see them paddling in a blow-up pool that's set up on the cool shade of the verandah. I want to dive into it, clothes and all, but the water's probably lukewarm already.

The tiny woman sitting to one side, splashing the kids, looks up with a toothy smile. 'Hello granddaughters.' She groans to a stand, wrapping her arms around me. I haven't been up to see her yet. Her giant-sized T-shirt and baggy shorts swallow me up in their folds.

'Hey Grams,' I say, kissing her damp cheek as she cuddles me into her arms.

'When'd you get ere bub?' she pulls back and looks me up and down. 'Ya need a good feed, ay?'

I smile. 'Bout an hour ago, just been at Aunty Barb's.'

'Mum sent us to watch the kids. She said you should come down for a yarn,' Candy says, from where she's tickling the littlies. 'They might ave a game a cards too.'

Grams's smile gets bigger. She squeezes me again. 'We'll catch up tomorrow, ay.'

I nod and she turns to shuffle inside.

'You fullas remember Raina, she's our cousin.' Candy draws my presence to the attention of their little group. She's already dipped her hands in the water and wet down her hair.

Katie smiles up at me, a soft shyness that says 'heartbreaker'. Tyrone shows off his own set of dimples, kicking his fat little body in his floaty.

I smile back but say nothing. Pain scrunches my chest, making my breath rattle. I'm used to being the youngest sibling. Now I'm the only child.

Grams comes back, carrying her smokes and lighter, a giant handbag slung over one shoulder. Her old pink thongs sparkle with bling.

'Alright you two. Ty's due for a bottle in an hour, and our little Kit Kat will be gettin hungry soon too.'

'Sorted.' I lift up the plastic bag and shake the GFC at her. She drops another quick kiss to my cheek as she passes.

'Have fun, kids.'

Eager for cards, she's in the car with Uncle Warren and they barrell away. Uncle Warren had sat patiently in his car that whole time. No one barks orders or gets impatient with Grams, not unless they want to talk to Gramps. Sweetest woman in the world, our grandmother. She married a man built like a tank who thought she hung the stars. Nick had his build. I push the thought away. She and Gramps are usually joined at the hip, and it was weird to see her without him. Must've been a good fight.

Water hits my face and I gasp; the cool shock feels awesome. I pretend to be pissed, grabbing up the food and marching into the house, my nose high. Katie and Candy's giggles follow me.

It's stinking hot inside, an oppressive stillness. Looking around, I can see every single window and door is open, but nothing stirs. I cross the lounge and hesitate in the doorway to the kitchen. For some reason, I expect to find someone standing in the room.

Shaking my head, I drop the bag in the fridge and head back outside to the others, where it's cooler and less suffocating.

We play the late afternoon away. Candy and I end up in the water, fully clothed. No one worries about togs around here. She fills me in on the gossip while we play underwater diving with Katie and push Tyrone around in his floaty.

The sun dips lower, bringing a tiny amount of relief. Both kids start to get cranky, so we haul them out and let them dry off on the warm wood. Candy gets towels for all of us. We dry fast.

This house is one of the old ones, meaning the bathroom is outside. It's not so much an outhouse as a cement block that looks like a public toilet. Inside is the laundry, and the only toilet and shower. It's not uncommon; houses like this were probably all built at the same time.

A lukewarm shower for the kids, and then Candy and I take turns having quick, pure cold ones. Candy lends me boxers and a singlet. We microwave the food and make chicken with chips and gravy sandwiches. Even Tyrone snacks on some, between pulls on his bottle.

Bellies full, I clean the kitchen while Candy settles the kids in the lounge. I can hear them fussing while she sets up a movie. Digging my hands into hot soapy water is the last thing I want to do. Sweat erupts all over my body, dripping from my forehead into my eyes. The sting distracts me for a second and I start, turning to stare at the empty hallway to my left. I could've sworn ... but I'm alone. I scoff at myself. Wiping down the bench and table, I hang up the cloth and almost jog into the lounge.

Candy's dragged in a foam mattress and two fans from the rat-warren of bedrooms slapped onto the house, need in mind more than interior design. She does the microwave popcorn while I lay out the junk food on the coffee table. Chips, Tristram's, chocolates, lollies. It reminds me of when I was little, and the older cousins would babysit us. Something warm blooms in my chest, knowing we're continuing a tradition.

We settle in, pulling the kids down to the mattress to snuggle.

We crank the fans to their highest volume, directing them over all of us as we wait for their film to finish.

Candy sniffs, then groans. 'Tyrone, already?' I laugh while she wobbles up with him in her arms. 'Keep goin, I'll change im right ere.'

'So we can sit in the smell of shit all night?'

She pokes her tongue out as she leaves the room. Katie was too engrossed in the story to register her sibling's departure. I'm lulled by the rush of air on my overheated skin. My eyes drift, wandering to the front door. All the doors and windows are still wide open. It leaves me feeling vulnerable, but everyone here does it. Only the odd car drives past, so it's not like anyone is around to watch us.

Burnt hills wave gently in the shimmering heat. The sun is sinking fast now, lengthening shadows and stringing the sky with reds and pinks. Darker blues push their way through them even now. The last of the light fades.

The hairs on my arms and legs prickle. A chill flows like a wave onto my skin. That feeling I had all afternoon, of being watched, intensifies.

'Whoo, he was putrid,' Candy laughs, carrying a snuggly Tyrone back in.

I try to shake the feeling. This is why I never watch horror movies. My imagination always gets the best of me.

Candy settles on the opposite side of the mattress, keeping Tyrone and Katie tucked between us. I sit up, pulling my knees to my chest.

'What's wrong?' she asks.

I shake my head. 'Whatchu wanna watch?'

'You choose.'

I pick up the top video, not even looking at what it is. Putting it in, I slip back to the bed and toss the remote to Candy. Snagging a bag of cheese and onion chips, I stuff my mouth with food to stop my fear leaking out.

By luck, I'd grabbed a family-friendly adventure. A fantasy. It should be carrying me away. But it feels like the tension is rising with the darkness. Despite the heat, I want to shut the doors and windows.

There's only so long you can stay ready like that. Especially when nothing happens. After a while, I relax back. The kids drift off to sleep, cuddling close to each other, Tyrone with his dummy and Katie with her thumb.

Cut the shit. The kids are fine. We're fine. It's all in your head.

Soft creaks make me jump and I look towards the kitchen. Candy laughs, 'You right cuz?'

I look at her, anxiety crawling across my face. 'This house . . . it's not . . .?'

I don't want to say the word. She shushes me anyway. 'Don't say it, you'll bring em.'

'Bring what?' I squeak. She winks and laughs. 'It's not funny,' I hiss. I probably imagined that nervous flick of her eyes.

'It's just a old house, it talks more than Grams does.' She waves me off, returning her eyes to the film.

Taking some deep breaths, I snatch some lollies, tossing a few at Candy's head. The brat catches them all. If there was something here, surely someone would've said. Every one of the mob loves to tell scary stories.

I shake my head, sliding down till my head hits the end of the couch. I pull the old sheet up to tuck it over my legs, like Grams always told us to do, to keep us safe. Candy chuckles and I shoot her the finger.

That's when I feel it, and I want to groan. I need to pee.

I try to push the discomfort away. But the movie isn't good enough to distract me from my own imagination, and it doesn't fare any better against pressing physical needs.

I can't even ask Candy to come. Someone has to stay with the kids.

This is stupid!

'Don't pause it.' I roll to my feet, marching out of the room. I pad through the darkened kitchen to the back door before the goosebumps catch me. Lights bring more heat and a ton of insects, so we haven't turned on a single one. It's full dark out there now. There's a torch by the back door for night-time trips. I snatch it up, flicking it here, there and everywhere as I slip down the stairs. There's no moon tonight, and no Milky Way to light the sky. There's a small breeze, but no relief from the heat. Away from the fans, I can feel the sweat building on my skin again.

It's less oppressive out here. But now I'm alone in the dark and about to pee in an old cement outhouse that's probably infested with cane toads. I move as fast as I can, while still checking for the ugly little suckers.

A quick look in the bowl and under the lid reassures me that no green frogs lurk, waiting to hop out at the worst possible moment. I relieve myself and wash up in the cement basin.

Mission accomplished, I'm feeling more confident as I head back. At the bottom of the steps, I pause. How could I possibly feel safer out here? But part of me doesn't want to look up at the doorway. Yanking in a breath, I bolt up the steps, running smack-bang into something soft.

'What the fuck?' I yelp.

'I need ta go too,' Candy laughs, taking the torch. Pausing, she blinds me with the beam, 'wait for me there, ay cuz?'

'The kids . . . '

'They're out to it. Just wait,' she grumps, dashing past me.

'Not like I have a bloody choice. I can't see a damn thing.'

My night vision ruined, I stay still, waiting. The soft glow of the movie comes through first. It's so still out here, nothing like the city. Only a few streetlights, no traffic noises. Just crickets calling in the dark, and the soft murmur of voices from the TV.

I can see the shadows of the table, chairs and kitchen cabinets. The entry to the hallway is a pitch-black portal. A scraping sound has me checking the doorway to the lounge. A sleep-eyed child doesn't appear.

Another sound: rolling on wood. This time I know it's from the hallway. My breath picks up.

I jump as a small shape skims into the kitchen. Too scared to move. It's a small ball.

Hands grab my sides. I dive forward with a scream. Candy doubles over, laughing so hard she can't even speak. I snatch the torch and whack her on the head with it. 'Bitch!'

She laughs harder as I point the torch into the hallway. Nothing but walls. Then down to what I realise is a cricket ball.

'Huh, how'd that get ere?' Candy steps forward, but I grab onto her arm.

'Wait, it . . . it just rolled out by itself.' She looks at me like I've lost it. 'I'm serious, it just appened.'

'It's a old house cuz, the floors slant. Things roll.'

I stand for a moment, but she doesn't look too keen to go pick it up now.

Dumping the torch back beside the door, I take off to the lounge. She hurries after me, sticking to my heels. The mad urge to laugh rises, but I choke it down.

Slouching back on the mattress, I look up at the screen.

Every hair on my body lifts.

'Did you . . .?'

'What?' she asks, fluffing up the pillow and shimmying into it.

'Did you leave the movie runnin?'

'Umm, hello?' she gestures to the TV, where the actors are frozen.

'That's not . . . I swear I heard . . . voices.' I look over and Candy looks further freaked.

'Don't be stupid,' she scoffs, but her voice is thready.

'But—'

'Look, stop fuckin around. Just shut up and watch the movie.' Candy points the remote.

A scene scrolls before me where the characters are kicking butt. Not a single word of dialogue to distract from the choreography and special effects.

No sign of the soft murmurs I'd heard.

I feel my heart pick up, match my breath.

That feeling of being watched creeps back. An urge to search the doorways and windows pulls at me. Like something is there, waiting to be acknowledged.

A loud click makes me jump. 'What was that?' I ask, staring across into Candy's eyes. Hers look almost as wide as mine.

'It . . . sounded like Mum and Dad's bedroom door.'

Sliding down further, I yank the sheet up to my chin. I flip to my side, curling my body around Katie's little frame. I don't care about the heat of being so close. I just have this urge: to protect, to hide.

Don't look, I whisper to myself, shutting my eyes.

'Dja wanna turn it off?' Candy asks me.

I shake my head. I wanted something to cover the sounds. Any sounds that shouldn't be there.

I thought she'd make fun of me. Waited for it.

I feel the mattress shift as she copies my pose, curling herself around Tyrone. I open my eyes to stare over their little heads into hers.

'It's just a old house,' she repeats. 'It's the tilted floors, or maybe a breeze?'

I nod. A breeze, that would do it.

'How long ya been in ere again?'

'A few days. We moved in just after Katie's birthday.' The place was normally filled with people. Teenagers, children, adults. Small sounds, little feelings, would get lost in the cacophony of life. The thought must've been clear on my face.

'No way,' Candy shook her head at me. 'If there was somethin in ere, Mum woulda felt it.'

A thud above us. I yank the sheet up over my head, forcing Candy to follow suit. We stare into each other's eyes.

'It's the roof coolin down. Old tin, no insulation, it did it at our old place too,' Candy says through a clenched jaw. 'Stop it, you're freakin me out.'

I nod. Not wanting to ask why she didn't pull the sheet down then. Cuddling in closer to Katie, I shut my eyes again.

There are long moments of nothing. The action scene fades and talking resumes on the screen. I focus on the words, drawing them in close. Reminding myself of the real world, where the paranormal and ghosts are just fiction. In the bright light of day, I'd probably laugh my arse off.

My heart slows. My breath steadies.

A growing embarrassment flushes my cheeks. Candy will tell everyone about how I've carried on. I'll be so shame.

I open my eyes to check what she's doing. Her skin is pale, tears leaking slowly from her eyes.

'What?' I mouth.

She shifts her eyes downwards, no other part of her body moving. At first I see nothing. Just the glow of the TV painting the linen in bright colours.

The light flickers. Something was moving between us and the light. Something that didn't make any noise on the bare wood floors.

My body tenses. I feel the tears well in my own eyes as I stare into my cousin's gaze. I struggle to quiet my breath, straining to hear. Anything.

The urge to lower the sheet is intense. Just a look. Something to prove that it was a trick of the light. A moth bouncing off the screen. Nothing.

If I look, all my fears will feel stupid. If I look. The elders say you should never look.

The air feels heavy, pressing down on us, but there's nothing there, I know it.

A growling hiss rises above the movie. Candy makes a tiny noise. Sweat slides down my forehead into my eyes.

It had been a man's voice, or an animal's. Sounded like it was coming from one of the rooms.

Our breaths pick up, fogging the space between us. I slowly reach out a hand to Candy. She grabs on like she's drowning.

A soft rolling sound, like someone moving that same ball down the hallway. Only this time in the opposite direction. Against the slanted floors.

The sweat between our fingers builds.

Another growl, closer this time. In the room.

I'm breathing so hard I feel like I'm going to suffocate. I desperately want fresh air.

What if it was a family member just fucking around? What if it wasn't?

God, please let Katie and Tyrone stay asleep.

I tighten my fingers on Candy's. I can feel her shaking. Know that I'm trembling just as hard.

Our world shrinks to that place under the sheet. I wonder if my feet are covered properly. Should I have tucked the ends in tight around me? Could something reach under them? I can't move to check.

A soft hiss. Air brushes the cloth near my neck.

The fabric shifts. Someone is picking at the edges at my back.

A pained growl in my ear wrings a sob out of me. Then running footsteps. Away from me. Out of the room, down the hall. A door slams.

I keep my eyes on the sheet stretched taut above us.

The pressure on the sheet lifts. The tension breaks. Candy and I relax our fingers. Something has changed, but what?

A smell like Lynx and football leather fills my nostrils. One I know and cherish, that's been missing for over a year. There's no way it can be real.

The TV light flickers and is partially blocked. A figure stands above us, its outline highlighted by blue shimmers from the screen.

Tears race down my face.

I know that build. Would recognise it anywhere.

A flicker and the shadow vanishes. The light returns. I yank the sheet down.

'Wait!' I sit up. There's nothing and no one to see.

Just us. Candy sits up too. 'Was that . . .?'

She takes one look at my face and climbs over the kids. Pulls me in close. I sob into her shoulder.

I don't let it go for too long. My grief for my brother would never end if I let it all out.

I pull away, dragging my shirt up over my face and scrubbing it, hard. Lowering it, I can see Candy staring around us.

All our junk food has been emptied onto the ground, the packets shredded like confetti. And we hadn't heard anything.

'Fuck this.' I shift Katie around, lifting her up into my arms. Burying her mumbling protest in my shoulder.

Candy reaches across, swooping up Tyrone. We're out the door that fast. Bare feet hitting wood on the verandah, then grass. We make it into the street, where the harsh bitumen pricks my feet. But there's no way I'm going back for my thongs.

Our pace slows to a walk. Never run, they reckon. It attracts things that will chase you.

We walk along the road, where the streetlights meet in the middle. As far away from the dark as we can get. There's no discussion, it's all instinct.

The urge to look behind chases me. One last pull. A quick glance. That's all.

I flick my eyes over my shoulder. A chill races over my body, blasting back the heat.

My feet pick up speed. I swear I'd seen a man's face in the windows. Watching.

I'm not going to look again to confirm it. If someone has broken in, they can take whatever the hell they want.

No one speaks. It's a bad idea to mention these things in the dark. It calls them to you.

We're two lone figures, walking in a strange silent world. The kids stay asleep. The dark lies either side of us. Watching.

No cars come along. No people move. No lights are on in the houses we pass. We could be alone in the world.

It takes just ten minutes to reach Aunty Barb's place. It takes an eternity.

The lights of Aunty's place finally come into view, warm and beckoning. I shift Katie closer to me. My arms are going numb.

The door is wide open. The adults are clustered around the table. Cards are flipping from hand to hand. Beers perch on top of a sheet that's stopping the cards from sliding off the table. It's all so normal.

We leave the streetlights behind and walk into the dark yard. Cane toads pop into my head, but I only hesitate for a moment. Our pace picks up across the dark space, desperate to reach the light.

We run into the lounge and everyone jerks around to stare.

'What the—' Grams calls. 'Don't come runnin in like that, you kids, you scared the shit out of us!'

Mum hops up, coming straight to me. 'Rain, what's wrong?'

I let her pull me close, her arms taking in both me and Katie. I'm shaking too hard to speak.

'Baby, talk to me.' Her voice is shrill now.

I stare over at Candy. She's in her dad's arms, her mum faffing around her, checking Tyrone's sleeping body. It's amazing neither kid woke through all of that.

Katie tenses in my arms, her little body tightening like an electric fence-line. Her soft wail brings Aunty Trina running and I gladly hand her over. Mum's arms never drop from around me. Katie's cries wake Tyrone, and the adults comfort them.

Mum drags me onto the couch, Dad taking up the other spot beside me. His gaze runs over us compulsively.

'Daught,' he demands, 'talk to us. What appened?'

My teeth are chattering despite the heat, but I force the story out as fast as I can. Stunned silence fills the space for a moment.

'It's that house.' Gramps' voice drags all eyes to him when I'm done. He stands in the kitchen, his arms around Grams, who looks just as shaken as I feel.

'I told you Katrina,' he snarls to his daughter. 'I told you not to move those kids in there.'

'But it felt fine earlier,' Grams protests.

He shook his head. 'You know better than that. You know what that place was.'

Mum's arms tighten around me. 'Dad, that's just a story.'

'My black arse.' His anger burns over me. Cleansing. I know that instinct, to fight fear and pain with the strength of rage. His eyes shift to take in me and Candy, their dark brown comforting. Mum's eyes.

Candy muffles her sobs into her mother's shoulder. Tyrone is safely tucked into Uncle Rick's arms, and she's pressed so tight to her mother, it's like she's five again.

'This is what comes from fuckin with things that don't belong,' Gramps growls at us.

'Gramps, please,' I whisper. 'What *was* that?'

'History, bub.' His face softens on mine. 'Reaching out to take hold again. That house used to be part of the old ospital. It was huge back in the gold-rush times. When the town got too small to need it, they chopped it up. Spread the old demountables around the whole town. New houses see?'

'But ... there was a ... a ball rolling, like somethin was playin,' Candy offers, looking up.

'Hmmm,' he nods. 'That used ta be the children's wing. Lotta sick kids back in them days. And it was where they'd take our kids. When we'd get too uppity. That's where they'd be put, to wait. Bad things appened in that ospital.'

'Dad, we been there a week, nothin as appened,' Aunty Trina protests.

He snorts. 'Bet that was the first time you left kids there alone. No adults to save them, see.'

Quiet descends. One filled with sadness and dread. I don't know what Aunty and Uncle will decide, but no way in hell am I going back inside that place. Not even to clean up the mess, or get my things.

'But that thing at the end,' Candy croaked. 'It helped us.'

Mum's hand strokes down my shoulder, pulling my eyes back to her.

'Not a *thing*,' she whispers, asking with her eyes what she can't bear to voice. Her face crumples when she sees the answer in my face.

We hold each other tighter. The pain of lost family piercing and deep. Always.

Nature Boy
(FOR MATT)

POPPY NWOSU

We lie side by side, my shoulder to his. Cool sand forms a mould around my body, as if I'm sinking. Despite the heat and mosquitos and the thick darkness, I feel at home. This beach is our place.

My brother points at the night sky. A stretch of stars taking over the whole world, and one star that moves. Coming closer.

'A spaceship?' he whispers.

I laugh as the wind picks up, ruffling my hair. Our parents are down the beach by the water, washing the pots and pans from dinner, baked beans burnt to the bottom of the billy can. They'll make coffee next, black, and sweet enough to make my teeth ache. Nearby, the flames from our campfire flicker and spark, light dancing orange across the sand. Across my brother's face.

'I don't believe in aliens,' I say. But the light in the sky is moving faster now, soaring close. It's big. Burning brighter than the stars and planets and black holes pin-pricking the vast space above.

My brother shifts on the sand. 'Why not?'

I shrug. Hard when you're lying down. 'Because I don't believe in anything I can't see.'

'You can see it right now,' he points out.

It's true. I think I can hear it too, like a hum inside my ears. A rumble in my chest.

Even though I know he's just teasing, I still get up and scream as the star bursts like fire overhead and the hum turns into a roar that vibrates my entire body. It shakes the sand beneath my pounding feet. My brother runs after me, yelling just as loud, and we both race down to the inky waves. Half delicious fear, half delight.

Our parents stand in the water, trousers rolled up to their knees and the sea licking salt into their skin. The water is black.

No moon tonight.

Dad rolls his eyes. 'What are you kids doing?'

I shrug, my chest heaving as I catch my breath. 'Just mucking around. Running from aliens.'

My brother laughs. 'You know. The usual.'

Mum frowns. 'It was a loud one though, wasn't it? I thought we came here for the peace and quiet.'

I shrug. I don't crave peace and quiet. But I do crave this place. The rising hills and the isolation. The milky way. This used to be a volcano, millions of years ago. Now it's a dark beach covered in surreal lava caves. Shapes rise from the black waves. The rock is petrified and hurts to touch, sharp as a blade beneath my hands.

I don't crave the endless wave of emergency planes that pass overhead, though. They carry water into the cane fields to douse the crackling fires.

The farmers light them every year, to flush out the animals ready for harvest. This summer though, they just kept on burning. The air is thick with sugar.

Now our isolated beach is a wash of activity. Emergency workers camping on their days off. Disaster tourists from the city come to watch the world burn. Politicians here to shake hands and look dour while they get their photos taken.

The fires aren't the worst, though.

It started around the same time. Only one or two people at first, but then more and more.

People began to unravel.

An impossible phenomenon, everyone says. And yet, no matter how impossible it is, it doesn't stop. Crowds protest it on the streets, set up research centres and foundations and helplines. Do anything to stop it. Sometimes it works. Sometimes it doesn't. Now everyone knows someone who knows someone impacted.

Soon, I will too.

Because at the end of this summer, my brother will unravel.

In the blue light of early morning, I step towards the churning water. My cousin tugs my arm, her feet crushing the patterns carved into the wet sand, bare toes destroying hours of creation by the tiny blue crabs that live here. She doesn't notice, just points towards the shadow rising from the sea, behemoth and bigger than my imagination.

Lava caves and rock formations loom from the waves too, but this new shape is different.

It breathes.

'See, I told you.' Flora stands close, her hand gripping my arm like a vice. The beach stretches long and flat in either direction as dawn creeps over the ocean, pink light and long dancing shadows receding from the hills. The sky is vast and streaked with red. Flora's hot breath tickles my neck as she asks, 'What is it?'

The shadow keeps breathing.

In.

Out.

Slow.

Laboured.

'It's a whale,' I answer finally, shaking my cousin off. We're the first ones to find it. Up with the dawn and barefoot on the sand, running wild here on the beach like I used to do with my brother. Being here during the anniversary without my parents feels like being sent away or turned invisible. Even though I was the one who insisted on coming.

I wish I hadn't now.

The whale lies heaving in the shallows, beached and rumbling, a monster of ribbed flesh and fatty tissue. The waves swirl around its fins and it sways with each crashing swell, driving deeper into the sand until its body has carved out a hollow filled with deep water. Its massive head is covered in knobs and barnacles. When it groans, the sand vibrates beneath my feet.

'What's it doing?' whispers Flora. Her eyes are wide, a sand-covered hand lifted to shade them. Other people are arriving onto the beach with the first light, emerging from their tents back behind the twisted trees. In the distance, two kangaroos move in a clumsy gait past the lava formations, down near the crashing waves.

I stare at the whale as the other campers gather round. Soon we are part of a crowd. 'I don't know,' I answer finally.

The noise from the gathering people grows so loud, I can't feel the whale's groaning under my feet anymore. Just the stomping and shuffling of arriving families and off-shift fireys. Everyone chatters and calls out, offering suggestions on what to do. A kid wades into the water as his mother shouts at him not to. He lays his palm flat against the massive beast's side; it rises and falls in time with the whale's laboured breath.

A woman next to Flora is lifting her phone into the sky, trying to call someone who can come and help. Who? Whale rescuers? I scowl. 'You won't get reception out here,' I tell her curtly.

Why is this place so crowded?

It wasn't this bad yesterday. Maybe more campers swarmed in from the city overnight, flying into the airfield and dodging the smoke from the simmering fires to find some sea breeze and escape.

Instead they found this heaving whale.

This beach used to be my family's place. Our secret. With its strange formations of rock and lush, curling rainforests, and the hidden trails up the mountainside to sweeping views over water and sky.

I glare at the woman and she glares back, still attempting to find reception bars on her phone. An older man beside her is talking about how the Dutch used to believe a beached whale was a sign of impending doom. The woman isn't listening, but I am.

'Impending doom of what?' I interrupt. Flora tugs on my arm, because she hates talking to strangers, and the beach is swelling with them now. I ignore her.

The man blinks at me. His face is puffy, covered with a sheen of sweat beneath his reflective sunglasses, even though the summer heat has barely set in for the day. 'What?'

I'm impatient. What does he mean, what? 'You said *doom*. Just now.'

'Doom?'

'Uh huh.' I'm getting worked up. It happens quicker these days. Maybe my patience unravelled alongside my brother. 'You said it's a sign! So I'm asking, a sign of what?'

He looks confused, until the woman with the phone interrupts. 'Ridiculous man.' She glares at him instead of me, then explains, '*Obviously*, he means a sign of the end of the world. Because of those internet cables, right? I heard that's what has been causing the fires and messing with the whales' sonar.'

Flora gasps but I roll my eyes.

Do whales even have sonar? I thought that was bats.

'Whatever,' I mutter, grabbing Flora's T-shirt because she looks like she's about to walk off after the couple, who are leaving now.

'It's a humpback, though,' I hear the man saying as they draw away. 'It must be the first time that's ever happened. You know the whales with teeth are the ones that beach themselves, not the whales with baleen.'

The couple move away down the beach, still muttering together and searching for reception bars. Both of them are wearing shoes, even though it's the middle of summer and the humidity is unbearable. The woman's have heels, sinking deep into the sand.

Flora stares after them, sweat beading on her upper lip. She squints against the sun. 'What's ba_een?'

I shrug. I don't know. I don't care.

A red haze glows over the volcano hills and smoke pours into the lightening sky over the lush rainforest. In the water, the whale slowly suffocates beneath its own weight, with a backdrop of heat lines shimmering in the humid air. I think maybe the world is melting.

The day draws on, long and hot, and Flora and I swim together in the shallows beside the whale. We walk the endless sand and explore the hidden lava caves, crawling on hands and knees into shadowy alcoves to sit alone in the dark. We trek beneath swaying palm fronds in the cool rainforest and eat a picnic overlooking a sweeping bay, watching as cloud shadows slide across the flat blue water and smoke rises from the burning fields in the distance.

All the while I feel it.

The tug of the dying whale.

It's like an ache in my throat or a thread lodged deep in my chest, calling me back to it.

By the time the sun slides down over the horizon, the crowd of people waiting on the beach has swollen three times in size. I don't even know where all these people have come from. But they are here to see the whale.

They take photos and pose beside it, while others use buckets to throw water and cool it down. Emergency workers push and shove it towards the rising waves, using vehicles and mammoth canvas straps in futile attempts to save it.

I stand watching in the gathering dark of twilight, on the wet sand alone. A hot wind ruffles my hair and billows my sweat-soaked T-shirt, and I hear the whale screaming beneath my skin, lodging deep inside my heart like a seed. I swear it is looking at me.

I stagger closer. Splashing into the waves. Close enough to see the whale's eye.

Big and brown.

I've seen eyes like that before. At the back of our old house behind the cane fields, beyond the shed with the ancient rusted harvester that looks like a brachiosaurus rising from the earth. Its shape silhouetted against a setting red sun. I walked there once. Alone. Ash from the cane fires floated from the sky and landed soft and delicate on my fingertips and tongue. I painted charcoal across my cheeks like war paint and slipped past rusted cages filled with growling cattle dogs.

It's where the abattoir lies. A gully with thick razor guinea grass, deep and dark beside an old tin shed. The earth was littered with cow heads, all rotted and decomposing in different ways. Some with ragged flesh still clinging to yellow skulls. Others collapsed inward, bursts of violent colour growing wild inside. Sweet-smelling thorned lantana bushes were taking over, their cloying scent mixing with the stink of rot.

One cow head was fully formed and perfect, like it had just been lopped off and laid down to rest on the thick grass. Black ants swarmed over the flesh and the air was thick with the stench.

I will always remember those eyes on that head.

Big and brown and sweet.

Like my brother's before he unravelled.

I stare back at the dying whale. At its big, soft eye.

Flora has gone to find her dad at the campsite but I cannot tear myself away. The water swells salty at my ankles and the humid breeze lifts hair from my sticky neck. The scent of frying sausages wafts from the campsite, beyond the break of twisted trees. Music wafts, too. A song about the greatest thing you'll ever learn. I listen to the faint drifting words until night sets in and the ocean turns black. The rushing wind beats back the acrid smoke from the cane fires, turning the salt air fresh with the lingering scent of ripe mangoes.

I breathe deep and long.

By the time I trudge up the sand to our camp, stars stretch overhead. And I carefully keep my back to the mammoth dying shadow with my brother's eyes.

I flop beside the campfire onto a carpet of crackling pine needles. They prick at the bare skin on my legs. 'What happens to people when they unravel?'

Flora gasps and glances quickly at her dad. We never talk about unravelling in our family. Especially not now, during the anniversary.

My uncle is sitting on a groaning canvas camp chair, with Flora perched on the esky by his side. Big, fat green ants crawl on the needles near her feet, but I don't say anything. Even when one climbs onto her big toe.

Uncle Jim looks uncomfortable, not meeting my eyes as he scratches his beard and shoves a crooked stick into the jumping flames. The piece of bread poked onto the sharp end turns black over the coals. 'Well . . . uh . . .' he says. And then falls silent.

I guess he doesn't know either.

'I heard it's literal,' says Flora in a hushed whisper. She leans forward on the esky with big, shining eyes, as if she's been dying for someone to ask her all day. All year, more likely. It occurs to me that Uncle Jim must have forbidden her from talking about it. Except now I've brought it up, so I guess that means it's open season on unravelling.

I suppose it's only natural. After all, it's impossible to look away from a disaster.

'I heard,' continues Flora, fluttering her hands wildly, 'that when you unravel, you come undone bit by bit. Like strips of skin just begin curling off your body and then you start coming loose. Like your organs fall out and your eyeballs and your intestines unwind, until there's nothing left of you but a big old pile of meat and blood and bone on the floor.'

I stare at her across the flames. Her face burns orange like the cane fires simmering in the distance, the red haze visible over the dark lava hills behind the campsite.

I am half-horrified, half-fascinated by her words. Is that what happened to my brother? Did he unwind and uncurl until he was nothing but a pile of guts on the floor?

I whisper, 'Where did you hear that?'

'A boy at school told me. He said it happened to his dad. One day, his dad came home from work and walked out into the back garden without a word and then he just . . . unravelled.' The fat green ant is crawling up Flora's leg now, almost at her knee. She still hasn't noticed. I watch it climb, my head swirling. Part of me wants to tell her to shut up. The other part wants to beg for more information.

Uncle Jim clears his throat before I can decide. He glances at me nervously and I expect him to change the subject, but maybe I look as desperate as I feel, leaning forward on the pine needles, eyes wide and hanging off Flora's words.

'You haven't looked this stuff up?' he asks softly. Carefully. As if I am fragile.

I turn away. 'Mum and Dad won't talk about it. And the internet is filled with . . . weird stuff. Like, I can't tell what's real and what's just rumours.'

Uncle Jim nods, thoughtfully. Then he surprises me by saying, 'I was told by a colleague that to unravel means to fade away. He says he saw it happen to someone in a parking lot. You know, one of those high-rise ones that go round and round and round? Up and up?'

I nod eagerly. I've been avoiding the topic so long, I didn't realise how hungry I am to know.

'Well,' begins Uncle Jim. 'My colleague says it starts at the toes. They just slowly fade away one by one, and the body turns translucent until you can see right through the person. Then they're gone. Just . . . poof.'

I whisper, 'Where do they go?'

'It's different whoever you ask,' he says slowly. 'Some people say heaven. Some don't. Depends on what you believe in, I guess.'

Flora interjects, 'Robbie said no one knows why it happens. Not even the top scientists. It just does.'

Uncle Jim shakes his head and readjusts his baseball cap. He hands me the burnt toast and places a sausage and onion into the space between the bread, squirting tomato sauce over the whole thing. Over my fingers too.

'I don't think that's quite accurate, kiddo,' he mumbles. 'I'm sure there's a reason. And lots of people are working hard on it.'

He stops talking, but both Flora and I are staring and waiting, so eventually he adds, 'Well, there's a lot of conjecture about it, obviously, and lots of theories. But it's not exactly an issue that can just be fixed, even if people do know what causes it. They say it's deep-set. Societal.'

'What does that even mean,' complains Flora with a wrinkled nose. The green ant is on her thigh now, near her resting elbow. I wonder which direction it will choose next.

'It means it's something no one really knows how to solve without upturning the way we live, the way we communicate, the way our society is structured and the pressures we place on each other.' Uncle Jim shrugs. 'I wouldn't even know how to begin. No one does.'

I'm silent, thinking for a moment, then I blurt, 'Do you think the whale is a sign that the world is ending?'

Uncle Jim chokes on his burnt toast, tomato sauce flecking into his wiry beard.

I shift closer over the pine needles, eager again. 'I mean, just, don't you think it's weird? All these unravellings and the cane fires that no one can put out and now this? A whale, here, on this particular beach . . . don't you think it means something?' I trail off.

I think maybe I sound crazy and now Uncle Jim is doing the thing grown-ups always do when they first hear that my brother unravelled. It's in his eyes, a certain look.

'No,' he says firmly. 'It doesn't mean anything. Sometimes things are just shit.'

Flora nods wisely. She's used to him swearing, but my parents never do, so I try to cover the fact that I flinched.

My cousin shifts the esky close to the fire, even though it's already so humid I'm sweating. She nearly up-ends the little travelling ant and it has to begin again from her ankle as she says, 'Everyone at school was talking about that.'

'About what?' Uncle Jim is eating again, mouth full and more red sauce in his beard.

'You know, like, the end of the world and stuff. Robbie says that it's all falling apart, the whole world, everything happening at once, you know? Like the fires and the unravellings.'

'Who's Robbie?'

Flora ignores her dad, voice turning hush. 'And now . . . it's the whales.'

'I don't think so, darlin',' interjects Uncle Jim. He's cooking more sausages, the scent of sizzling onions filling the air and mixing with the salt of the ocean and the sweet pine needles.

Flora just shrugs. 'Robbie reckons it all means the world is ending. I reckon he might be right.'

I shiver despite the heat and glance into the thick wall of darkness that marks the edge of the beach, where the firelight can't reach.

It's out there. The giant.

Still breathing.

Still slowly dying.

I swear I can feel it singing inside my chest, calling to me. Out there in the night, just a shadow among the black waves, oily surf swirling and pounding against its swaying body.

Uncle Jim's voice snaps me back.

'Bad stuff has happened before in the world. And it'll happen again. People just forget, that's all. We all only live one lifetime, and no one learns anything from history.' He sighs. 'Bad stuff piling up worldwide doesn't mean it's all ending.'

'It does!' Flora insists. The green ant is back on her knee. 'The whales are beaching themselves all over the world, in all these different countries. It must mean something. Something really bad is happening, Dad. It's like that dude on the beach said, you know, about electricity and that new internet cable . . .'

I wrinkle my nose. Uncle Jim must be thinking the same thing as me because he scoffs. 'An internet cable? Those conspiracy nuts. They think those fires started because of a cable? It's climate change! The world is getting hotter all the time.' He pauses, mouth full. 'Or was it cooler? I can't remember.'

'Hotter,' I say. I'm distracted. By the ant crawling in circles on my cousin's leg and also by memories of my brother. Rippling through my mind. Until last year, we lived in a tiny town nearby, nestled in a village surrounded by cane fields and bursting rainforest. From my backyard, I could see waterfalls shining silver down the mountainside.

My brother and I melted into that landscape. It was home.

But when he unravelled, my parents couldn't bear to live there anymore, so we packed up, closed in, shut down and moved everything away to the nearest town. A mining community filled with people with too much money and nothing to spend it on.

Without my brother around, my parents didn't want to visit this isolated beach with its surreal lava caves and artwork strewn across the sand by tiny blue crabs.

I did, though. I wanted it so badly that Uncle Jim offered to take me.

But now I'm here, none of it feels the same.

'I can't believe that whale is just going to unravel like this,' sniffs Flora.

I freeze, staring at her with the breath wiped from my body. The world grows thick as molasses. Closer and smaller and stifling. Flames burst and crackle, sparks dancing into the night sky.

I attempt to suck in air. 'What did you just say?'

My cousin frowns and Uncle Jim keeps munching his dinner. I've finished mine and my fingers are slick with grease. Flora stares back at me. 'The whales that beach themselves, they unravel . . . didn't you know? It's been on the news every night.'

I shake my head slowly. I cannot breathe. Cannot think.

My cousin adds loudly, 'I heard they're the only animals that unravel, right Dad?'

'Sshh, Flora,' my uncle warns, hand on her arm and eyes on me. 'Let's give it a rest now, okay?'

Slowly, I drag myself to my feet. The wind picks up and I stare through the trees towards the ocean. Its black out there, shadows curling and swelling, the wind wavering over the branches. People still gather on the beach in the dark. Buckets of salty water are still being thrown over the whale that has my brother's eyes.

I watch the dark but can't go down there.

I want to know but I don't.

I want to see but I don't.

I want . . . something. And I want it desperately.

In the end, I don't venture out into the dark to find it,

whatever it is. I stay huddled by the fire with my family instead. And I reach over to Flora and flick the green ant from her leg. She gasps gratefully and douses herself with bug spray, while I tell a story about how if you eat the bum of a green ant it tastes real sweet, like honey on your tongue. I laugh at the sour face she pulls.

Uncle Jim watches us and grins. He plays that same song as we get ready for bed, turned down soft on a little neon glowing player. Some old crooner from the 1940s singing about the greatest thing I'll ever learn. I only half listen.

We go to bed, all three of us cramped into one small tent, falling asleep while listening to the waves on the shore and Uncle Jim's soft music, the same song over and over until the recording clicks off. I imagine the ocean licking salt into the barnacles and crustaceans growing on my whale's ridged skin.

It dies slowly on the sand, crushed beneath its own weight, as I lie awake and wonder what it would feel like to unravel.

The world is still shrouded in night when I wake.

I slide from the tent, trying not to make much noise, because my cousin and uncle are still sleeping. Flora is breathing soft and her chest rises and falls in a rhythm like the beat of the waves. She's only a little younger than me, but it feels like a lifetime these days. I don't know why.

The remains of the fire have turned to charcoal. I lean down in the almost-dawn darkness and press my fingers to the ash, draw it across my face like war paint. I don't know why I do that either.

I do a lot of things I don't understand these days.

Stepping barefoot over the dirt of our campsite, I nudge a blackened billycan lightly with my toe. Green ants scatter across the ground. I wrinkle my nose.

My uncle doesn't know anything about camping. He doesn't understand that you need to clean the pots straight away before the ants come in droves. He doesn't know that you can't leave a sausage unguarded if you don't want it snatched by a kookaburra. He isn't even aware that you have to keep your esky locked in the car, because the turkeys and kangaroos will get into it otherwise.

Plastic wrappers and ripped bread-bags scatter around my feet in the dirt.

I suppose I could have told my uncle those things.

But I was distracted. And maybe a little bit angry.

Maybe I'll tell him next time, even if this place is different now. Not how it was.

In the deep night, I walk barefoot down the beach. The sand is hard and ridged with carved patterns beneath my feet, wet and cool despite the humid air. I taste salt on my tongue.

Overhead, the moon shines pale light onto the water, dancing shapes over the waves and across the heaving whale. I creep silent as a ghost between the sleeping people strewn across the sand, all of them resting soundly on towels and doused in chemical mosquito spray. They've lingered here to help the whale live, or watch the whale die, or maybe, like me, they're drawn here because they want to know what an unravelling looks like.

I can feel it will happen soon. A tug in my chest. An ache.

A need to be beside it.

I wade into the waves. No one on the beach stirs.

I feel like the only person for miles and miles.

I heard a whale can drown at high tide, but the ocean barely reaches my humpback's fins. It has carved a deep cavern in the sand, sloshing wild water and storming waves as it heaves, swaying back and forth.

Dying slow.

The inky water swells to my knees, moving like oil, colours reflected pale from the moon above. I'm careful not to stumble, but the ocean slides up my legs and soaks my clothes. I can breathe fine, head well above the surface, but it still feels like drowning.

The dark presses inwards as I kneel at the whale's side, water rising to my chin and dripping from my hair. Salt inside my mouth and eyes. I press tentative fingers, slick and wet, against the whale's side. It feels like rubber beneath my hands, bumpy and fleshy and firm, all at the same time.

I can feel it beating and living beneath my fingertips. The whale's skin is burning.

I think this is it.

The moment of unravelling.

I wonder if it will dissolve into a bathtub of blood and flesh and slimy animal guts, with a stink like those discarded cow carcasses from the abattoir? Or will it simply fade away noiselessly, and cease to be?

What will the whale feel as it unravels?

Does it know that it is leaving?

I am crying now, the tears sliding down my cheeks mixing with the seawater. I wet my face until I'm soaked through and dripping. I am the ocean and the ocean is me. The whale is my brother and my brother is the whale.

I know it isn't true, but I dream it into being anyway, because I miss him.

Swaying in the water and nudged by the rising tide, I lean close to the whale's big, soft eye. The skin around it is smooth, marked by age and stained with old barnacles, long since worn away. The eyeball is as big as my fist, bigger. White around a deep, dark pupil.

I stare at the whale and it stares back.

Water sloshes around my body, the salt scent strong. The whale is burning. Changing. I am crying, humming the song Uncle Jim always plays on repeat. I can't remember the words but I sing it anyway, and I don't know if it helps or makes things worse.

But I am here.

And maybe that is enough.

The beast shivers, great shudders crawling across its heaving, giant body as tiny shapes form over the spine. At first, I think they are new barnacles, pushing out into the night air. They break skin and part bone until they protrude from the whale, strange shapes rising in silhouette against the moon and deep ocean beyond. But then something erupts near my hand. The heaving flesh pushes out a flower. Bright yellow balls of pollen, delicate and intricate. Growing wild.

Yellow wattle.

I breathe deep and the sweet floral scent settles above the salt smell as more and more sprigs of bright yellow burst through the whale's shivering skin. Banksia grows where the barnacles used to be. Eucalypt leaves sprout from its vast chin. Moss grows on the whale's fins and scraggly red bottlebrush flames from its mouth. A tangle of palm fronds creep like vines along the soft underside as the whale collapses inwards. A jumble of growing things, sprouting leaves and bright splashes of colour. Grevillea and lilly pilly and kangaroo paw, all showering onto the ocean's surface until I stand in a widening pool of flowers. The air smells sweet.

I remember the last line of the song now.

So I sing it softly beneath my breath as the whale unravels beneath my fingertips, its eye blooming into a pale, delicate rainforest orchid, no longer seeing me. Flowers and leaves float in the ocean, swirling in the soft waves beneath the moonlight. When the tide changes, they will all be washed out to sea.

And I will remain here.

Slaughterhouse Boys

EMMA OSBORNE

The cow's screaming cuts through the noise of the party. The celebration carries on, all bitter beers and squealing rock music and blue singlets, and the only thing Tom can do is smile until his cheeks hurt and rub his thumb over the hilt of the knife at his belt.

By the end of the night, the cow's blood will coat his tongue.

If Tom was brave, he'd leave. He'd drive until the car ran out of petrol, he'd run until his legs gave out, he'd crawl until his knees bled.

But he's here. This whole night is for him. Everyone's here to celebrate his killing, and to watch the recording of him killing the cow who was unfortunate enough to be called his.

'Come on, come and eat!' His dad's voice echoes through the house over the noise of the cow on the screen. He's out the back, slapping bloody meat around on the barbecue. There's rump and chuck steak for the others, but they've kept the prime cuts for the birthday boy. The eye fillet. A porterhouse. Some of the cow will be frozen and saved for special occasions. His twenty-first, his thirtieth. Maybe his wedding. The rest of the flesh is here, to be cooked and claimed, mouthful by mouthful, by his hungry, angry family.

Tom doesn't want it: not the meat, and not the life it will baptise him into.

'Tom! Get the fuck out here!' His dad yells.

Tom can't pretend that he didn't hear, but he can delay. He holds up his empty beer bottle – Coopers Pale – and swirls it so the yeast leavings swoop through the dregs. It's a rough beer for a rough man, but all he feels is weak and cowardly.

Maybe the blood will give him strength.

Outside, the music blaring from an old stereo switches to an AC/DC song and everyone whoops through the opening riff. They lift their drinks to the sky and throw their heads back. The neighbours won't complain tonight. Everyone in town knows what day it is, if they're not here already.

Tom walks through the house like a rat down a snake's throat: slow and deliberate. He swipes a fresh beer from a plastic tub filled with ice in the kitchen and allows his tall, sweaty Uncle Mick to smash a heavy palm down on his back.

'You're a man now, Tommy-boy. A killer!' Mick laughs, that big stupid laugh, and his blue singlet strains.

'That's it!' Tom tries for enthusiastic, but the anxiety leaks through. He will need to eat soon.

'Thank god you're not like fucking Pete,' shouts his dad's mate Johnny from across the lounge room. His mates are always up for a free feed, especially since the die-out tripled prices.

'Fucking Pete!' Uncle Mick replies. He spits right on the floor of the kitchen. 'Coward.'

Pete, the boy next-door, took his cow money and went. He didn't have to make the kill, and he didn't have to spend his sixteenth birthday with his family, with a steak shoved down his throat. Pete got out, but he'll pay. His family will never speak to him again.

'You got a girl?' Uncle Mick passes him a stubbie holder from the back pocket of his jeans.

'Got a couple,' Tom lies, swigging his beer. Mick laughs again at that, conspiratorial, approving. If only he knew.

'Well, I don't see anyone on your arm tonight? What about Kristy's mate? The American?' Mick inclines his head at Tom's cousin and her mate, who are picking through a box of records in the lounge. 'If I was ten years younger . . .'

Tom fakes a knowing laugh and necks the rest of his Coopers in one go. It burns his throat. He grabs another beer out of the tub. Yesterday he was fifteen and it's still not legal for him to drink, but tonight he's a killer, a man, and they're unlimited for him.

The only thing he wants is Pete.

Pete called Tom a dozen times during the week before his birthday. Sent fifty texts. None of them answered. Tom could have called him any time, and Pete would have driven over, picked him up, maybe kissed him, run his fingers through his hair. Taken him away, and fed him something made from plants. They could have gotten away together.

But Tom didn't call him. He couldn't. He drove three hours in the heat and the dust to kill his cow instead.

He knocks his beer against Uncle Mick's and they both drink deep. They're poor as shit, but his dad always finds money for beer. And they've all saved for years for the cow. Tom has cleaned trucks, spent hot and sweaty hours building fences, driving steel stakes into the baked earth. He's folded boxes at the pizza shop until the tough cardboard shredded his fingers. He's scrubbed toilets and sticky pub floors. All of the pay went into the cow fund, unless his dad was feeling generous and passed on a twenty. For incentive. Poverty is the best incentive in the world.

There are some boys who can eat meat whenever they like. Rich boys, who have a stockyard and a butcher. They've never seen a live cow, never watched it kick and buck in terror. Their meat comes on bone china, is cut and cooked tenderly for their soft mouths.

Poor boys spend their childhoods dreaming of real meat. And when they turn sixteen, they take a knife down to the yard to make the kill with their own two hands. They wear clothes they can't spare. Their mothers wash out the blood when they get home with cold water, harsh soap.

Rich boys don't work. They have everything paid for: clothes and music lessons and real animal flesh. Poor boys and their families spend what could have been a university fund on one cow. One cow to kill and eat, to share with family; a bloody respite from protein blocks and chemical flavours that can only mimic the real thing.

Rich boys can say no, and their families will understand.

All through the house on shitty old TVs, the cow – Tom's cow – is slipping around in the dust. It bashes its heavy body against the pen. It's lowing frantically, trying to get away. Tom detaches himself from his Uncle Mick, goes into the lounge. He watches himself stalk the cow across the pen, watches himself unclip the knife from his belt. He drinks again to hide the tears pricking his eyes.

Tom wishes with his heart, his hands, his breath, that he'd thrown away the goddamn knife. Never mind that it's an heirloom and that he should feel lucky it's his to pick up.

His cousin Kristy didn't flinch. She was made for killing, made for blood. She should have the knife, really. But he can't give it away, not now. Kristy and her dark-haired friend have abandoned the records and are standing around a table in the lounge. They're drinking something bright orange that reeks of cheap vodka.

'Tom! Where the fuck are you?' his dad yells through the open window.

'I'm just catching up with Kristy and her mate!' Tom replies, and his dad just winks at him.

His dad wouldn't dream of dragging him away from a pretty girl, because what could be more perfect than his favourite boy killing his beast and getting his first fuck all in one night?

He doesn't know that Pete was Tom's first. And he never will.

'You gonna eat?' Kristy asks, all tall and bleached-blonde and perfect. She's snipping meat off the bone of a fatty chop with her incisors. She's two years older than Tom and had the whole family with her, watching, when she made her kill. Tom's heard his dad say that he wishes Kristy were his daughter.

'Yeah, yeah, I just wanted to come say hi,' Tom says, holding his beer tight to stop the shake of his hands. 'What's your name, then?' he asks the friend, because he knows that people are watching.

'Connie.' Her accent is American, and she's looking at the party like she wants to be sick. 'Is there anything to eat around here that wasn't once a sentient creature?'

'Aunty Jill has some chips, I think,' says Kristy, licking her teeth. 'Maybe some noodles?' She points to Tom's mum, who is sitting alone in the tiny dining room. Jill sits with her back as stiff as the plastic fork she jabs into her bowl of two-minute noodles. She's drinking wine out of a box and refills her plastic champagne flute the instant she finishes. When the music picks up and throbs through the floorboards, she closes her eyes softly for a moment, but doesn't get up to turn it down.

'I'm just going to head back to yours, Kristy,' Connie says, hugging her hands around her elbows. 'See what's open in town, maybe get a pizza.'

'I'll grab a cab with you,' Kristy says, a smear of grease around her lips. 'The guys are disgusting around here.' She stares at Tom, who wants to say, no, it's not like that; I just needed to talk to someone to get away from my fucking family. I don't even like girls, I—

'Can't you take it?' Tom asks Connie, amping up the swagger in his voice. He'd beg her for a ride if he could. 'It's how we do things here. Kill for the family. No real meat unless you kill it with your own two hands. But I bet in America it's different? Easier?'

Connie blanches. Tom knows that America is essentially dead, that she's likely a refugee. He shouldn't fuck with her. But he's scared, and hassling her is a distraction.

'You don't have to be an arsehole, Tom, god. How many beers have you had?' Kristy spits with the fire that his father loves.

'Sorry,' he says, ashamed. 'It's a big day, you know. See you at Christmas, Kris.'

'Whatever.' She and Connie stalk off.

Tom watches them go, stops himself from calling out.

The cow video starts again on the lounge-room TV.

On the screen, Tom looks tough and capable, but the definition isn't good enough to see the tears tracking through the dust on his cheeks as he moves closer to the cow. Its eyes are rolling as it hops uncertainly from side to side. Tom can't get the thought out of his head that the cow's brown eyes look almost human. Frightened. It twists away, shakes its short horns.

It's smart enough to know what's coming.

Tom knew too, but now it's too late.

His young cousins thump around the house, meat juices dripping down their chins as they chew on raw hamburger mince. It's probably their first taste of the real thing. Something to be treasured.

Tom finds his way through the crowded porch and snags a paper plate off the picnic table. The bass thumps into his already-tight belly. Someone is pissing on the side of the house. Tom can smell hot fat, burnt onions.

People are clustered around flaming steel drums, the coals licking their faces with orange light. The men are hairy and rough-voiced; the women dirty-blonde, their thick woollen jackets like armour. The women laugh loudly, cutting through the drums and the pop of guns in the distance. The battered stereo switches over to a Rolling Stones song. One of the old guys, Jimmy, is fucked-up drunk and keeps walking, tripping, pushing to get to his car. A bunch of people are shouting at him, trying to get him to sit down before he falls down. Jimmy doesn't listen. He just keeps heaving toward his car, undeterred.

Tom looks out over the yard. The dark goes forever beyond

the bug-dotted lights. Empty paddocks and bush beyond. Nothing to stop him if he stole some car keys and just went.

The dark is quiet. It asks him for nothing. It won't tell him what to eat, or who to love.

Someone's dropped a sausage and stepped on it with boots on, grinding gravel fragments into the mushy innards. Maybe tomorrow someone will pick it up, scrape off the grit, and eat it anyway. In his childhood, there'd always been a dog around to eat anything that slipped off a plate, but nobody here can afford a dog, let alone the food for it.

'There he is!' His dad is thrilled tonight. 'There's my big man! Come here and eat your steak.'

Now they're all looking at him, and some of them are cheering and screaming. There's another TV on the porch, in case he thought he could get away from the footage. It must have played a hundred times tonight, all through the house. There is no escape from the cow's kicking. On the recording, an attendant steps forward with a cattle prod and shocks the cow until it drops to its knees and then falls. Tom leans down to cut its throat. Even sharp, the thin knife struggles on the cowhide, and Tom ducks around the thrashing hooves. Something intangible bleeds out of his heart as he cuts. Something essential.

Everyone at the party laughs and screams as the cow dies. Then they skip the footage back so that they can play it again. Soak in the killing. His aunts and uncles and cousins and all of his dad's mates are louder than the Collingwood cheer squad on a crucial siren. Louder than all of their cars put together, louder than death.

'Thanks, Tommy!' they yell, not knowing what it cost.

His dad pushes him into the chair at the head of the outdoor table. There are still broken Christmas lights strung up across the yard with wire. Fleeing is no longer an option.

Tom has a platter thrust at him, a fork plunked down at one side. The platter is loaded with a thick rib steak. The charred crust is reassuring until he realises how much thin blood has pooled underneath.

One by one, his family and his dad's mates turn away from the TV and the cow that's dead on the ground that is now cut up and dotting white paper plates around the yard. Everyone wants to watch him eat the only tenderloin he'll ever taste, and the only meat he'll get unless a cousin makes the kill. They want to celebrate him, to thunder his triumph to the cold black sky. Maybe if he eats, they'll love him. Maybe enough to forgive him for the thrill of lust he feels when he thinks about the dusty boys from town, about Pete.

Maybe he'll belong.

His mother stands behind them all, up on the porch, her eyes low. Tom knows that she loves him, but her love alone is not enough.

Tom draws his knife and looks down at the meat. The blade is serrated along the back and is wickedly sharp. He'll just eat it once, just tonight. Tomorrow he'll go back to protein blocks. He'll scrub the blood off his ruined shorts. He'll finally call Pete.

His family holler as he pins down the steak with his fork. It oozes a little, juicy and rare. He cuts off a slice, smaller than what it would have been if it were a government-issued protein block. Quickly, before he can change his mind, he flips the shred of pink meat into his mouth.

He wants it to be disgusting, sick, repellent. He sees the cow kicking in his mind. Dying, for him.

He bites down and the juices flood over his tongue. The meat is salty, rich, and delicious. He groans.

Tom thought he'd hate it, but the meat tastes so goddamn good. It tastes better than Pete's kisses, his sweat.

'Nothing like your first mouthful of something like this,' says his father. 'I'm proud of you, you know?'

And that's what does it.

Tom cuts another mouthful.

The flesh is fatty and the charred parts crunch under his teeth. Tom eats until he's gorged, until his lips are smeared with grease. His belly protests and he thinks that maybe it'll rebel later, but right now, all he can think about is the meat. His family crow as he dips a finger into the pooled blood on his empty plate. He licks the blood off his fingertip, barely stops himself from licking the plate.

I'm sorry, Pete.

There's relief in his father's eyes, his shoulders, as the family all keep drinking, all watch Tom reach for another chunk, all swallow down bloody meat themselves.

They're so happy and so very proud.

This is not the kind of love that Tom wants, not forever, but it's here, now. And true. Heavy in his stomach.

Tom claims their love, soaks in it.

Just once. Just tonight.

Euryhaline

MARGOT MCGOVERN

I won my first swimming race years before I laid eyes on a pool. Nan says I'm precocious. Mum calls it ambitious. Truth is, there aren't any competition-size pools on the Yorke Peninsula. In Innesburgh we learn to swim in the sea. But even among our community of fishing families and oyster farmers, I always had an unusual affinity for the water, and after I became the youngest person to swim across the bay at high tide, a rumour went around that I was part mer.

Perhaps that's why the Milford pool unnerves me. From my dorm-room window, the water sits so flat and achingly blue inside the glass-walled swim centre that it hardly seems real. It's an intelligent pool, according to the school website. Capable of chemical regulation and equipped with cutting-edge performance monitoring systems.

'Bit of a step up from the old Innesburgh tidal pool,' Mum says, dropping my duffle bag on the floor to join me at the window and pulling me in for one of her bone-crushing hugs. 'I'm proud of you, Tam.'

I squeeze her back and catch sight of something dark jetting beneath the pool's surface. The shape resolves itself into a girl as she rises for air. She hasn't bothered with a swimming cap. Her dark hair moves behind her, fanning then slickening over her pale back. My pulse ticks up as I see how fast she moves.

'Tamsin?'

Mum steps back, and I realise I'm gripping her shirt.

'Sorry,' I mutter, letting go.

'Will you be alright here?' She scrutinises my face and a worry-line creases the smooth skin between her eyes. I force myself to take deeper breaths. *Steady.*

'If Milford's a bad fit, you can always come home.'

Part of me wants to take her up on the offer, climb back into our dusty ute and make the three-hour journey back to Innesburgh. But I already know what waits for me there, and the Milford scholarship is the escape ticket I've been working for. So I smile, bright as I can manage, as the girl in the pool executes a perfect turn in the corner of my eye. 'I'll be fine.'

'I have something for you.' Mum fusses in her overlarge handbag. I cross my fingers for extra pocket money, but she presents me with a caterers' box of salt.

I stare at it, confused. 'Thanks—?'

'For protection. Remember when you were little, I'd pour a line of salt along your windowsill before bed—?'

'To keep out ghosts from the wrecks. It's been years since I had those dreams, Mum.'

'I know.' Mum takes a final, appraising glance around my room. 'Just something to remind you of home.'

After Mum leaves, I want to swim. My limbs are restless from the long car ride, and I'm keen to test the pool before the first squad training tomorrow afternoon, but the dark-haired girl is still doing laps, staking her claim with each slicing stroke. So I shelve the idea and set about unpacking. My dorm room is bisected by an invisible line, identical furnishings on either side: narrow bed, wardrobe, desk and a nightstand that doubles as a locker for valuables. There's no sign of my roommate yet, so I claim the bed with the better view of the pool and take my time settling in, fussing over the folding of T-shirts and socks, arranging and rearranging the books on my desk to draw out the task over dinner. My thoughts drift as I work, following Mum's ute back along the Yorke and St Vincent Highways, past wheat fields and salt lakes to the squat shack we share with Nan on the Innes Bay shore. I won't miss the town, but I ache for the grey-green tumult of the sea and the salt-rough winds gusting in off the shoals. They haven't prepared me for the stillness here, where tall pines block the breeze and the air is smoky and dry with the memory of summer fires. As night sets in, I secret Mum's gift in my bedside locker behind my chocolate stash and tampons, and fall asleep listening for absent waves.

I wake to the sound of breathing. For a moment I can't place myself, and the furniture shapes crouch like watchful figures until I spy a glint of blue beyond the window. As my eyes adjust, the shapes resolve to ordinariness: wardrobe, desk and a girl in the other bed. She's turned away from me, her dark hair combed slick and her pillow damp beneath, as though she couldn't be bothered with the hairdryer after her shower. Her breath catches on each intake, like the soft suck of a skimmer-box flap. It's hard to tell with so little light, but she might be the girl from the pool.

'Hey,' I whisper. 'You awake?'

The girl doesn't reply and after a moment it becomes uncomfortable to keep watching her. But I remain aware of her presence at my back, the steady rasp of breath keeping me awake until the shadows start to thin. When my alarm sounds I'm sure I haven't slept, but I must have, because my roommate is already up and gone for the day: her bed as neatly made as it had been the previous afternoon.

The swim centre is empty when I arrive, but the air vibrates with the hum of the pool's mechanics. It makes the place feel inhabited. As though the pool itself were a presence. This is the first time I've seen it up close, and though I've studied its specifications – in-ground, eight-lane, Olympic-size – the scale of it still makes me catch my breath. It's a broad sweep of crystalline blue, shockingly bright in the muted dawn. I've never seen water so still. So controlled. The hum seems to intensify, inviting me closer. I step to the edge in a kind of daze, half-believing I could walk from the tiles clear across the pool's glassy surface. But the illusion shatters the instant my toe touches the water and sends widening ripples across the pool. The drain splutters with the disturbance, and I startle at the sound. My foot slips and I'm plunged down, down, down, in a tumble of piercing blue.

I've barely registered that I'm in the pool – that I, swimming champion given a free ride to this ridiculously luxe school based solely on my mastery of water, have *fallen in* – before something small and black comes scuttling towards me. I scream and kick up, water filling my lungs as the thing zips beneath me, just missing my ankle. I surface, gasping, and grope for the side.

'Gotta watch the tiles. They're slipperier than you expect.'

I look up, chlorine stinging my eyes, to see a frizzy-haired girl about my age wearing a Milford tracksuit, swim bag in one hand and goggles swinging in the other.

'There's something under the water,' I choke. 'It came at me!'

'A camera. They're motion-activated. Takes some getting used to.'

I'd read about the cameras. Milford's secret weapon. They track along the bottom of each lane beneath the swimmer, recording their laps so the coaches can better analyse their performance. Each one costs a fortune. Most Olympic hopefuls don't get to train with that level of technology.

And I almost broke one.

On my first day.

Because I thought it was attacking me.

'Could this maybe stay between us?' I venture.

'Sure thing, wunderkind,' the girl replies with a teasing smile. 'You're Tamsin Stewart, right?'

I feel like I'm sinking, even though I'm out of the pool. 'How'd you know?'

'Coach said the under-seventeens open-water state champ was joining us. I did my research.' She sticks out her hand. 'Izzy Ellis, Junior Swim Captain. I was going to get in a few laps before first lesson but . . . breakfast?'.

The dining hall is chaotic with the clamour of three hundred girls reuniting with their friends and I'm grateful to be walking in with Izzy.

'Izzy! *Izzy!*,' a voice calls above the din. *'ISOBELLE ELLIS SMELLS LIKE LETTUCE!'*

'Sunita!' Izzy's smile breaks wide as she guides me through the melee towards a broad-shouldered girl waving her arms at us.

They hug and perform a complicated handshake, talking over the top of one another until Izzy remembers me standing awkwardly beside her.

'Tamsin Stewart, meet Sunita Biswas.'

'The new girl from Innesburgh, right?' Sunita looks me over with an appraising eye as she kicks out a chair for me. 'My uncle has a farm near Yorketown. My cousins used to take me scavenging at Innes Bay.' She turns to Izzy. 'The rockpools are full of old nails and glass washed in from shipwrecks that happened, like, *hundreds* of years ago.'

Izzy raises an eyebrow. 'For real?'

I nod, thinking of the *Ethel*'s rust-rotted ribs jutting through the sand a little way down the coast, and the stories of drowning sailors thrust up on the sand, babbling about silver-tailed rescuers.

'Strange place,' Sunita says with a look that implies that I, being from said place, am also under suspicion of strangeness. 'Is it true you scored the single in Gilman? Room G6?'

For the first time that morning, Izzy's smile slips. 'You're in Camille Lyon's old room?'

'I guess. Why? Who's she?' I ask.

The girls exchange a look.

'Former teammate,' Izzy says. 'She doesn't go here anymore.'

'Yeah, because she had a meltdown.'

'She was *overwhelmed*, Sunita.' Izzy turns to me. 'It happens sometimes. There's a lot of pressure. Not everyone copes.'

I wonder if she means it as a challenge. Back home, I'd imagined my scholarship as the grand prize from which my happily-ever-after would naturally flow. Now I'm beginning to see it for what it is: a place in a more competitive race.

'Camille was a freak, Iz.' Sunita shovels a mouthful of eggs and, lowering her voice, beckons me closer. 'She thought the pool was evil. Said the water was polluting her blood. Rumour has it, she tried to bleed the toxins out.'

'*Sunita.*'

I close my eyes against the image that comes. *Breathe, Tam, breathe.*

'All I'm saying is that I wouldn't want to sleep alone in that room after her. Even if it meant having a single.'

'I have a roommate,' I correct. 'She's on the swim team, or she should be. Long, dark hair? Really good form?'

Both girls stare at me blankly and Izzy shrugs. 'Must be another newbie. I guess we'll meet her at training.' She watches me scratch my arms. 'You got fleas?'

'I think it's the chlorine.' I had a rinse after my fall, but my skin still feels itchy and slightly sticky. 'We don't swim in it at home.'

'Hope you're not allergic.' Sunita covers her mouth and laughs. 'Could you imagine?'

'Is that a thing?' I ask, worried.

'Um, *yeah*. Gives you a horrible rash, like you've been bitten all over by mozzies. Itches like crazy too.'

'But you're probably not allergic,' Izzy assures me. 'The coaches are paranoid about things spreading through the water and putting us out of commission, or worse, giving Milford a bad name. They've programmed the pool to up its anti-bacterial defences when it senses something new in the water.'

'So technically it *is* poisoning you. Just like Camille said.' Sunita waggles her eyebrows at me. 'Creepy right?'

'Ignore her. You just need to acclimatise. What do you call those fish that live in both the sea and fresh water?'

A word rises from past biology lessons. 'Euryhaline?'

'That's it,' Izzy grins. 'Be euryhaline, wunderkind.'

I keep Izzy's advice in mind at our first training that afternoon. We begin with scratch races so that the coaches can see which squad veterans have kept up their form over the break, and figure where the newbies fit. The old girls toss cocky taunts to their friends as we mount the starting blocks, but the mood is tense beneath their posturing. More than a few cast hard glances my way and I focus on drawing each breath into my lungs. All day, I've been thinking about Camille Lyon and her belief that the pool is malignant. Logically, I'm certain it must have been the pressure of Milford twisting her thinking. But when I catch sight of the camera watching me beneath the water, it sends a shiver over my skin.

I'm determined to prove to myself and my teammates that I'm worthy of my place here. When the whistle sounds, I fix my sights on the lane ahead and dive. As an open-water swimmer, my strength lies in knowing how to read and navigate the ocean's fickle moods. But the pool offers no resistance, the water parting before me with each stroke like warm oil. It should be an advantage. Instead, it's as though I'm riding a bike stuck in too low a gear: working hard and getting nowhere. The pack breaks at the twenty-five-metre mark, leaving me with the stragglers. I try to adjust my technique, controlling what elements I can: the timing of my breath, the motion of my legs, the angle of my arm as my hand scoops the water.

Kick, kick, pull.

Kick, kick, pull.

Breathe.

Kick, kick, pull.

Kick, kick—

But each time I look down, the camera is keeping pace. It makes me self-conscious, and I overthink what I'm doing.

Breathe, Tam, breathe.

I'm splashing too much. Sloppy, my coach back home would call it. And as the wall looms up, I know I've fumbled my first impression. My time flashes on the screen above: fourth place. Not bad, but not good enough.

I haul myself from the water and bury my face in my towel, waiting for my shaking breath to steady.

Izzy follows me out of the pool, pulling off her goggles as she squats beside me.

'You okay, Tam?' Her face is creased with concern.

I try to reply and find I'm crying.

She rubs reassuring circles over my back while our coaches and teammates give us a wide berth, pretending not to see.

'It's only a scratch race,' she assures me. 'It doesn't count.'

But later when we make for the showers, the head coach taps my shoulder and takes me aside.

'What happened out there?'

I shrug, watching the pool resettle itself over her shoulder as the last swimmers climb out.

'I'll write it off as first-day jitters,' she offers. 'But, Tam?'

'Yes, Coach?'

She fixes me with a level stare. 'We brought you here to win.'

Shame burns beneath my skin, and the chemical taste of the pool is still in my throat as I head back to the boarding house. Even though I'm hungry after training, I skip dinner for a second night. There's no sign of my roommate when I get in and I realise that she wasn't at training either. In fact, there's no laptop or books on her desk. No trinkets on the nightstand. I hesitate a moment before the wardrobe on her side of the room and my thudding heart tells me what I'll find before I open it: nothing but a few wire coat hangers. Whatever I saw in my room last night wasn't a girl. I put it down to a bad dream, conjured by nerves, and make an exhausted attempt at my homework. But my gaze keeps drifting back to the empty bed. Later, as

I'm packing away my books, I look out at the pool and see the dark-haired girl gliding through the water with a naiad's easy grace. I take the box of salt from my nightstand and sprinkle a line along my windowsill as I watch her swim, to keep the nasties out.

With our first meet less than a month away, we train before and after school every day, with lunchtime gym sessions and cross training three times a week. Saturdays are for scratch races, with a viewing party Saturday night where the coaches critique our footage. On Sundays, we try to catch up on homework and sleep, but there's an unspoken understanding that we'll also find time to run a lap of the cross-country track. There are daily weigh-ins, meal plans, stress tests and physicals. It's no wonder the other schools don't stand a chance against us.

The constant observation and evaluation makes me nervy and the naiad, as I've begun to think of her, swims her way into my dreams. She beckons from outside my room, her hair wet and hanging in her face so that only one eye is visible: the pupil glassed and beady as a camera lens, edged in piercing cyan. The first time it happens, I wake to discover my window open. When I move to close it, I find a ring of damp splodges on the concrete walk below and the line of salt broken on the sill, as though dissolved by damp hands.

The dreams make me wary of the water. My stomach knots in the hours before training and the air catches in my throat before each dive. But the smarting shame of my first fumbled scratch race returns whenever I'm tempted to skip a swim, and

Coach's admonishment is a constant echo in my thoughts: *We brought you here to win.* So I push myself to adapt. To be, as Izzy suggested, euryhaline. I swim through every spare hour, refining my technique and learning to cleave a cleaner path through the water until I'm certain that if I cut my palm, I'd bleed Milford blue.

I swim as though my life depends on it, because, in a way, it does. I never fit in with the kids at home. When I won the open-water championship, they left half-rotted fish stinking at our door and poured water through my schoolbag, soaking my books and ruining a laptop we couldn't afford to replace. When no one was around to see, I'd gather fish scales from Mum's gutting table and stick them on my legs with a wet finger so that when I sat just so and squinted, they fused to a single, fleshy fin. I imagined swimming clear of the bay, the powerful flick of my tail carrying me beyond the wrecking shoals and across the gulf to the possibilities beyond. On bad days, I set my sights on the shoals and swam until my courage gave out. Nan reckons it was this off-with-the-fairies thinking that got the other kids looking at me funny to begin with, but Mum says the day we stop knocking on the backs of wardrobes and clapping for fairies is the day we might as well give up altogether. 'Insist on your cup of stars,' she used to say with a dreamy look, quoting Shirley Jackson. And she's right, I think. Better in the long run to seek the improbable. But with mermaids and fairies and possible worlds come ghosts that tap at windows, and shadowed figures crouched in corners. Sometimes I wish I couldn't see them. And that quote? I looked it up; it comes from a haunted place.

When I call home, Mum answers on the second ring.

'Tam! How's my mermaid doing?'

Her voice crackles over the burr of gulf wind and I picture her on the beach, looking across the water to the invisible spot on the horizon where she knows me to be.

'You've had me and Nan worried, ignoring our calls.' Her voice is bright with false cheer, as though my silence were a minor thing, but I hear the hurt beneath.

'Sorry, Mum. I'm always in class or swimming.'

'And busy with new friends?' she asks, hopefully.

I think of Izzy and Sunita and wonder whether they count. Izzy's kind to everyone and bullies Sunita to be the same. They save me a place at meals and cheer for me at training. But sometimes I catch Sunita making a private face at Izzy over something I've said. It makes me wonder whether either of them truly likes me, or if they see it as their swim-squad duty to make me welcome. 'Something like that.'

'Are you doing okay, Tam? You sound husky.'

'I didn't sleep well.'

There's an uncertain pause on her end. 'Bad dreams?' And when I don't reply. 'Are you using the salt, Tam?'

'That's just superstition.'

She drops her voice and I can barely hear her over the gusting wind. 'Do you need me to come get you?'

I imagine returning to my old school, praying each night that I'd wake too sick to go, eating sandwiches alone on the edge of the salt pan behind the gym where no one thinks to look. I can't go back to that. I won't make it out a second time. 'I'm good,

Mum. I'll call more often.' I force a smile into my voice and look at the pool through the window, ignoring the crunch of salt on the carpet beneath my feet. 'You don't need to worry about me.'

Soon after the call with Mum, I start putting extra salt on my meals. Just a sprinkle at first, and a teaspoon or two in my water bottle. To ease the dread knotted in my gut. I feel the crystals moving through my blood as I swim, making me shine. Keeping me safe. My times improve. But exhaustion muddles the line between days and dreams. Time twists and I lose track of what assignments are due and where I'm supposed to be. Only the date of our first meet feels fixed: a black hole sucking all my effort and energy.

I swim after lights-out. Honing my technique. Shaving millisecond after millisecond off my best time. Increasingly, I sense the naiad at my back, her pale hands grasping at my feet as I power through the water. I'm too scared to slow down or look back, and she's gone from the pool when I finish my laps. But later, in the showers, I discover scratch marks on my ankles and clumps of dark hair clogging the drain. I skip meals. First out of forgetfulness, then by design. Each mouthful is a stone in my belly, weighing me down. Making me easier to catch. I drink salt water instead: I crave the sharp sting on my tongue. The rasping swallow. The pain feels good. Purifying. Sparks dance behind my eyes, so I know the magic's working.

I think I'm doing well, until there's a knock at my door in the middle of the night and Izzy comes in to yank up the blind.

'Tam?'

I squint against the mid-morning sun. ' 'Msleeping.'

'At recess? You skipped training yesterday and this morning. The coaches are worried – we all are . . .' Her voice trails off as she takes in the state of my room: two weeks' dirty laundry lumped on my absent roommate's bed, damp towels strewn on the floor. Salt glinting on the carpet beneath the window and in a ring around my bed. 'Are you okay?'

'Just tired.'

'Maybe you should see the nurse,' she ventures. 'You look sick.'

'It's the chlorine. I'm still having a reaction.'

'Right,' she says, but doesn't sound convinced. 'I know it's hard when you first arrive here – I cried most days my first term – but you can't miss classes and training. Not with the first meet next week.'

And not on a scholarship.

'I know when the meet is, Izzy,' I snap.

She startles at my tone and I expect her to give up and leave, but she sits on the edge of my bed and looks out at the pool. 'I've seen you swimming at night. You're fast when you think no one's watching.'

I think of the naiad's hook-like nails grasping at my heels. 'Not fast enough.'

'It's your attitude. Sunita and the others swim as though they're leading, even when they're not. You, on the other hand, swim like you're being chased.' Izzy pushes off the blanket and takes firm hold of my leg so we can both see the scabs on my ankle, and the long-healed scars beneath. 'This isn't an allergy, Tam. Get your head right, or this place will break you.'

I pull the blind again when Izzy leaves so I don't have to watch the naiad swimming laps. That afternoon I put an extra handful of salt in my drink bottle and head back to training. The coaches give me the same concerned look as Izzy, but welcome me back and even offer a few words of encouragement when I win the day's scratch race. If I seem nervier than usual, that's to be expected: the whole squad is on edge in the days leading up to the meet. There's no more talk of my seeing the nurse. The coaches' jobs, like my place at Milford, are contingent on us winning.

The day of the meet, I'm light as sea foam and my thoughts shimmer blue. I could fly high or gust away, depending which direction the wind blows. I rub my skin with fistfuls of salt until my blood rushes to the surface and takes the magic in. I've soaked my swimmers in salt water too. The crystals have dried into the fabric, so that when I glimpse my reflection I see my mer-self, scrubbed and shimmering. The salt's charm sees me through the heats. I'm placed in lane four for the fifty-metre freestyle: the race favourite. Izzy is beside me in lane five. As we wait to be called to our marks, she takes my hand and gives it a squeeze.

'See you on the podium, wunderkind.'

But the heats have dissolved my salty armour, and I twitch beneath the crowd's collective gaze. *We brought you here to win.* The tiles list and lilt beneath my feet. *Breathe, Tam, breathe.* A cheer goes up as we step onto the start blocks and I curl my toes into the rubber grip to keep my balance. With each thud of my heart, my vision narrows until there is only the thin blue ribbon of water before me. My muscles coil in readiness, and I tuck my head between the V of my arms as I take my mark. Somewhere below, I feel the lane camera adjusting its focus as the pool registers my presence. The race official raises her whistle and an expectant hush falls over the pool. It's so quiet I can hear the gargled suck, suck, suck of something caught in the drain. *Focus, Tam,* I tell myself. But a dark shape plumes beneath the water's surface. The lane line, distorted by ripples. Or my eyes playing tricks. The start whistle shrieks and my body, conditioned by years of training, launches into the pool. But in the split second before I dive, I see – or think I see – a dark sop of hair hanging from the skimmer-box.

Panic seizes my chest, shocking the air from my lungs as the water closes over me. I kick for the surface, blinded by the churning swell as the other swimmers pull ahead. My lungs burn as I give chase and the camera tracks below, its eye swivelling back as the thing in the skimmer-box slips into the lane behind me.

Kick, kick, pull.

Kick, kick, pull.

Breathe.

Kick, kick, pull.

Kick, kick, pull.

Breathe.

Terror propels me to the head of the pack as we pass the twenty-five-metre mark. But I feel the naiad gaining, the water sucking at my heels as she darts towards me. The crowd roars, in terror or encouragement I can't tell, and my heart beats so hard it hurts. A dozen more strokes, a few more seconds, and I'll be out of the pool.

Kick, kick, pull.

Kick, kick, pull.

The camera swivels its focus back to me. Or follows the naiad as she closes in.

Kick, kick, pull.

Kick, kick—

Something wisps across my belly as a dark shape glides beneath me.

Breathe, Tam, breathe.

Hair, black as lane tiles, billows into the neighbouring lanes. I scrabble for the surface, gasping for air and choking on water.

'I can't— I can't—'

Ahead, I see Izzy slap her timing pad. The crowd erupts, but the cheers and applause are cut short by urgent whistle blasts ordering everyone out of the pool. I circle my arms in a desperate effort to keep my head above water as the naiad's hair becomes a great, spreading darkness, filling the pool and knotting around my legs and torso to pull me down into the widening void.

I hear my name and turn to see Izzy's face distorted in fear as Sunita drags her away from the edge. Our head coach is yelling, her voice firm and authoritative, but I can't make out the words. She throws a kickboard on a rope and I understand: my distress is a dangerous thing.

I swim for the board, fighting against the binding knots. But everyone is watching me now and the collective weight of their stares pushes me back beneath the surface, into a dark, paralysing place where there is only the suck, suck, suck of widening drains and glassed, cyan eyes watching me sink.

And I can't breathe.

Tentacles of hair twist up my nose and down my throat.

I can't breathe.

The strands knot and tighten in my lungs, squeezing out the air.

I can't breathe.

White flecks of lingering salt magic spark across my vision. I look up to the shimmering surface and hear my teammates calling my name as the darkness tightens around me, dreadknots holding me in place.

I can't—

But I try. Lungs burning and heart raging, I struggle towards the kickboard floating above.

Kick, kick, pull.

 Kick, kick, pull.

My fingers slap the plastic.

 I can't—

Slipping.

 I can't—

Gripping.

 Breathe.

Hunger

MARIANNA SHEK

I didn't force her to eat the apple. She practically stole it. Plucked it right out of the fruit bowl sitting on the mahogany buffet in my living room. Maybe the lack of sugar from her latest diet clouded her judgement. She didn't see the statue of the red-faced, pissed-off Guan Gong, the Taoist god of war, glaring down at her from behind the bowl. Two other deities stood on either side of the golden warrior. They wielded curved broadswords and dripped 24-carat bling (my mum accessorised her statues more than my little sister did her Barbie dolls). Completing the tableau was a stone incense burner – the remnant of incense coil still smouldering, a matching pair of red lamps shaped like candles, and a photo frame of my great-great (great?) grandparents.

To be fair, Carrie was neither Taoist nor Asian. Still, it was a little culturally tone-deaf not to recognise that this was some sort of shrine.

My parents transferred me to All Saints College at the beginning of the year because they thought it would give me more opportunities. The school might as well be called All Whites. Five Asian students in a cohort of one thousand. (Two of them, my sister and me.) No wonder I'd been keeping a low profile. Not making trouble, but not making friends either.

Carrie was the exception. We met at auditions for orchestra.

'You'll never play well on a Stentor,' she told me.

I didn't believe her until she was appointed first chair violinist. After that, she took me under her wing.

Today, she'd come over to my house to help me learn a new piece for orchestra. My fingers couldn't slide over the strings fast enough and I was going slightly off-pitch.

'Relax your neck or you'll ruin your posture.' Carrie sounded so much like my mum that I reacted instinctively. My arm twitched and my bow jabbed at her eye. Luckily, the doom-laden tune of the *Castlevania* opening credits blasted from her phone at that moment and she ducked to fish it out of her bag. My bow sliced harmlessly through the air, in the empty space where her eye had been.

'Be right back.' A bright smile crossed her face. I knew it was Dean, her gamer boyfriend. He was the only person in her address book with a customised ringtone. Love is lame.

As soon as she left, I grabbed a handful of salt and vinegar chips. Then, I picked up my violin again, my greasy fingers marking the battered wood.

Carrie's voice carried down the hallway. 'Looks like I won't be able to watch your tournament tonight, babe. Christina needs a lot of help . . .'

My bow bounced across the E string, causing a screech. Carrie hated watching Dean play *Resident Hell*. Once, at a party, we played the game. Carrie shrieked at every jump scare and mashed all the controller buttons. I panicked at the final boss stage and gave up my turn to Dean.

'. . . Well, Mr Minchin said he would drop Christina if she didn't improve . . . you remember Christina? She went to your party . . .'

Screw this. Band practice was over. I stretched out the crick in my neck as I trod down the hallway. Carrie whirled around, a smile pasted on her face and an apple in her hand, its shiny surface marred by a bite mark the shape of her perfect teeth.

'Where did you get that—?' My gaze shifted from Carrie to the pyramid of fruit on the shrine behind her.

'Sorry, I'm starved.' She devoured the fruit in five bites. Fruit my mother had lovingly arranged for my capricious ancestors. She wiped her sticky chin with the back of her hand. The hairs on the back of my neck prickled.

'Something wrong?'

I was on the spot. Carrie had welcomed me into her circle of Cool Girls because being 'woke' includes having at least one hanger-on from a minority race. Occasionally, she even joined me for a boba tea (so long as it was zero sugar, which defeated the purpose of the drink if you ask me). She had dipped into multiculturalism. That didn't mean she was ready to hear that she'd awoken a horde of hungry ghosts.

'I just remembered I told my mum I'd help my sister with her homework.' I wished I'd thought of a better lie as soon as the words left my mouth.

'You overheard me talking to Dean?' Carrie's cheeks flushed. 'Don't worry about it. I'd rather hang out here with you.'

'No, I really have to help Michelle.' I shooed her towards the door. 'Dean's tournament sounds fun. Tell him I said hi. Let's take a raincheck on the practice.'

'I've got to get my violin!'

'I'll bring it to school tomorrow. Have a good night.'

Carrie's lips fixed in a pout as I shut the door. There was no time to explain that I was looking out for her best interests. And mine. Without her, my position in the orchestra would be jeopardised and the invitations to parties would dry up. I raced towards the back shed to perform the one ritual that could save us.

The combination lock on the door is three-eight-eight. Mum reckons the lucky numbers have saved us from being robbed. I think no thief wants to tackle my parents' hoard. In the twenty years since they migrated to Australia, they hadn't thrown out a single thing. Holding my breath against the stench of mothballs, I wove my way around red-white-and-blue striped jumbo bags stuffed with old clothes and DVD racks piled high with Hong Kong dramas, until I reached a bulging cardboard box.

The scent of sandalwood hit me as I peeled back the flaps. Inside were stacks of fake paper money designed like Monopoly bills, from a Hungry Ghost Festival special edition. Hell money for ghosts to use in the afterlife. Underneath the bundles of $10,000 notes were the more traditional joss papers, made of flimsy paper pulp, a square of gold or silver stamped into the middle. I snatched a handful of notes and pressed them to my rabbiting heart.

My sister Michelle appeared at the door. 'What are you doing?'

'Making an offering to the ancestors to undo a curse.'

'You just want to set something on fire, you pyro. I'm going to tell Mum you're not studying.' She ran back to the house, probably to work on some mathematical algorithm that she absolutely did not need my help with. I only got accepted into All Saints because Michelle won an academic scholarship. An older sibling should help the younger one get into the desirable school, not the other way around. It was a family 'joke' that Mum never tired of recycling.

Wasting no time, I dumped my supplies near the barbecue in the courtyard. My parents finished work in an hour and if they saw me burning paper money to the grandfolks, they would know something bad had happened.

I layered thick brown cardboard to form an offering basket. It took some time to fold the traditional joss paper into gold and silver nuggets. On top of this, I generously piled on the hell money. And, to be certain I'd be pleasing my ancestors, I added two old Scratch-It lottery tickets – according to my mum, they were fierce gamblers.

The wind blew out my first two strikes of the match. On the third attempt, a spark caught on the corner of a hell note. It curled black around the edges, then – *whoosh!* – the entire bundle lit up. Nervously, I poked at the paper with tongs, willing it to burn faster. My eyes stung from the smoke. I wondered if I should grab my lab glasses.

'You got anything smaller than $10,000?' asked a husky voice.

On the faded plastic sun lounge lay a wizened old woman in a frayed blue tunic and hemp pants. She crossed her matchstick-thin legs and held up the bank note as if inspecting it for watermarks. No longer charred, it had acquired a pearly sheen. 'No offence, but it's hard to get change for $10,000 for a packet of cigarettes.'

I bowed my head in what I hoped looked like a show of respect. 'Thank you for looking after me, great, great . . . great grandmother. I hope my offering will ease your suffering and I'll try to remember to bring you some loose change next time.'

'Oh, call me Granny Wu,' she chuckled. 'Aiya! You got my flat nose. Which one are you? I can't keep track of all my descendants and their requests.'

'I'm Christina, Jenny Wu's eldest daughter. I'm not here for myself. A friend of mine, Carrie, accidentally ate fruit from the family shrine. She didn't mean to be disrespectful.'

'Then why isn't she kowtowing? Didn't want to risk blistering her pretty fingers lighting a joss stick?' Granny Wu's scrawny hand disappeared up her sleeve and scratched vigorously. Flakes of dry skin fell like confetti. 'Bad luck for her,' she continued. 'But what can I do for you? You want me to fix an exam?'

Could she really do that? I was a solid B-grade student, which wouldn't bother me so much if Michelle wasn't always showing me up. 'Isn't that cheating?' I asked.

'Kids these days are so PC. Cosmic nepotism isn't cheating.' She tucked the money into her tunic. 'What about boy troubles? I can help with that.'

Dating opportunities are slim in an all-girls school. The only guys I knew were through Carrie's boyfriend. Gamers with pale skin and terrible posture. All of them, except for Dean. I thought about the firm way his hands had taken the Xbox controller from me, the intense look on his face as he timed the Lightmare sword to save me from the demon king.

Granny Wu smiled knowingly.

I blushed. 'Look, if you really want to help, please don't torment Carrie. She's my friend.'

'Was it the Fuji apple she took?'

A second ghost, much younger and fatter than Grandma Wu, suddenly appeared in the other lounge chair. Cicadas crawled from the hem of his black silk robe and landed on the pavers. 'That girl ate every last morsel and licked her fingers afterwards.'

'No one asked you, Hong Zi.' Granny flicked a cicada off her shoulder.

He glared at me resentfully, his chubby fingers pulling at the mandarin collar around his neck. Underneath the fat rolls was the hint of a chin.

'The Fuji apples are my favourite,' he muttered.

'Glutton! Get out of here!' Granny Wu slapped his head.

I didn't feel any better when he disappeared. Could he pop up wherever he wanted? What if he appeared at Carrie's house right now?

'Don't worry about your Uncle Hong Zi. He's a dog, but I've got him on a leash.'

'And my other . . . relatives?' I asked. 'You'll keep them away from Carrie as well?'

Granny Wu brought a card up to her nose and inhaled deeply. It took me a second to realise it was the scratch game I'd burnt as an offering. 'Aiya! Barely enough here to tickle the nose hairs. What is this – a $2 bet? You gotta take risks to get ahead in life.'

'I'm only fifteen. The ticket was my dad's.'

'Wu women always marry cautious men. Common swifts who play dead at the sound of danger.' She looked at me slyly. 'Which one are you, Christina? A swift or an eagle?'

If I said an eagle, she'd know I was lying. I stared down at the ground. The trail of cicadas had disappeared, leaving only husks.

Granny Wu smiled. She was missing her eye tooth. 'Your

head's hollow, your heart's thumping and your gut led you to me. Oh, there's plenty I can do for you. Next time you come to visit, bring something of a little more value, Christina.' She flickered like a YouTube video when the internet cut out, then disappeared completely. All that was left was the scratch-card on the lounge chair and the smell of burnt charcoal.

The A-note resonated throughout the concert hall. The violinists and cellists picked up the pitch and the woodwinds chimed in. I fumbled open my violin case, grabbed the bow and raced to join the orchestra just as they finished tuning. Mr Minchin, the conductor, glanced up hopefully when I climbed onstage but went back to rearranging his score as I pushed past three second violinists to get to my seat.

Behind me, the flutes twittered madly.

'Thanks for making Mr Minchin wait,' I whispered to my neighbour, Sonya.

'We're waiting for Carrie.' She frowned and nodded at the empty throne closest to Mr Minchin.

My stomach twisted in knots. Carrie had never missed a practice. I didn't even know if she was in school today.

'Enough chatter, girls.' Mr Minchin rapped his baton on the stand. 'Let's start with the final section of the William Tell Overture.'

The opening bars of the piece relied on a strong brass section. Mr Minchin's baton cut through the air as I stared at Carrie's empty seat.

'Violins!' He turned towards us.

I tucked my instrument under my chin. For once, my finger placement was perfect. My bow bounced lightly off the string, producing the tone Carrie had been struggling to teach me. I glanced up. Mr Minchin inclined his head ever so slightly.

I got the hint. Pay attention to the next section coming up. This was an extremely quick passage that required a separate bow-stroke for each note. Fast pieces usually make my hand cramp, but today, my wrist folded over the fret. I felt light as freshly risen dough. Paganini couldn't have raced over the fingerboard any faster. Beside me, Sonya had lost track of where we were on the score and even the first violinists were sounding scratchy.

'Stop stop stop! Everyone, listen. Christina's got it right.' Mr Minchin made me repeat the passage. My first solo in the orchestra.

Be cool. Be cool. There was no need for a fist-pump just because I nailed it.

'Christina, come and sit with the first violins.' Mr Minchin tapped Carrie's empty seat, the concertmaster position. 'Let's go from the top.'

That night, I rearranged the fruit bowl into tropical food art: a pineapple centrepiece, surrounded by star fruits, lychees, even a couple of Fuji apples. I added extra coils to the incense burner until the scent of sandalwood fogged my brain. Even when I escaped to my bedroom, the incense burned into my dreams.

Carrie was gorging on a custard apple, smearing the milky pulp over her lips and chin. 'It's a new diet and face mask in one. You should try it, Christina.' She held out a fistful of mushy flesh. I reached out with my hand, then recoiled as something twitched in her cheeks. The shiny black seeds had turned into burrowing scarab beetles, their scrabbling legs like the cicadas that had crawled from Uncle Hong Zi's hemline.

I awoke to the stench of foetid fruit. Over breakfast, Michelle stared down at her cereal, red-eyed and sniffling, while our parents talked about us like we weren't in the room.

'You want to spend money on a tutor?' Dad frowned at the piece of paper in front of him. My sister's carefully crafted algebraic equations weren't balancing against his pay cheque, not with the heavily scored B on top of the page.

'What can we do?' Mum snapped. 'You want her to lose her scholarship? Turn out like Christina?'

'I pulled an A-minus in my last maths exam,' I told them.

'Mind your own business!' Michelle started sobbing in earnest. I almost felt bad for her. Was it my fault? All I'd done was light joss sticks and make fruit art. I never explicitly asked Granny Wu to hurt my sister.

My phone vibrated. It was a good excuse to leave the table.

'Christina?' The voice on the other end was familiar, male, urgent.

'Hi Dean!' I chirped, then winced at my eagerness.

'Have you heard from Carrie?' Dean laughed nervously. 'There've been the craziest rumours. Someone said she was in hospital with . . . some kind of food poisoning? Which is weird, because she's so careful about what she eats.'

This can't be a coincidence. First my promotion in the orchestra. Then Michelle failed maths. And now Carrie, hospitalised. Granny Wu was teasing me.

'Is she seriously hurt?'

'That's what I'm trying to find out!' Dean sounded frustrated. 'Her mum won't tell me anything. Carrie said her family likes you. I'm hoping if we go to her house together, they might tell us something.'

'Sure, I'll go with you!'

'Thanks.' A high-pitched whine like laser fire from an eight-bit game cut through the speaker. 'Sorry, I'm practising my combos. I've got a tournament tonight. Hey, you like *Resident Hell*, don't you? Want to come watch? Afterwards, we can see her family.'

The back of my throat and nose tingled. At the dining table, my parents and sister were still arguing. No one had moved. So why could I smell sandalwood as intensely as if someone had lit fresh incense?

Carrie didn't return to school the next week. In trigonometry class, Dr Reedy called out her name on the roll.

'Her parents told me she wasn't coming back for the rest of the term,' I volunteered.

'Hey Christina, is it true her parents checked her into Headspace Clinic?' Sonya asked.

I hung my head but didn't answer. The room broke out in murmurs, part-serious, part-gleeful, the sort of hushed tone we used when talking about eating disorders.

'Everyone, open your homework,' Dr Reedy said sharply.

'Miss Muso finally hits bass.' Sonya glanced sideways at me so I forced a grin. 'A bunch of us are going semi-formal dress shopping this afternoon,' she whispered. 'Want to come?'

'Sorry. Can't. I'm hanging out with Dean.'

'Carrie's cute boyfriend?' There was no judgement in her voice. If anything, she sounded a little awed.

I nodded.

'Cool.'

How did gamer girls dress? I owned jeans instead of short skirts, blouses instead of ironic T-shirts that no one really understood. If only I was the Claudia Kishi kind of Asian instead of a Lane Kim nerd. Dean was meeting me for coffee in half an hour and nothing in my wardrobe was good enough. I got down on my knees to trawl under my bed. As I reached for a crumpled cardigan, my knees scraped against something sharp.

With a hiss, I recoiled. Something had scratched the wooden floorboards so viciously that tiny splinters had pierced through my clothes. Bright spots of blood blossomed on my denim knees.

Mum and Dad were going to freak. Michelle must have finally sneaked a dog into the house. Then I saw the rice trail. Dry white pellets wound around the bedpost to my desk, where I found a small cluster, like a pile of dead maggots, behind the bin.

I leaned on my desk until the dizzy spell passed. This wasn't the work of an animal. A hungry ghost had been in my room. Watching me sleep . . . sniffing about . . . touching my things. I snatched my hand off the desk as if it were contaminated.

When the 8-bit drone of *Castlevania* erupted from my phone, I nearly jumped out of my skin.

'Hey Christina,' Dean chirped. 'Carrie called me!'

'What?' I was still distracted. 'I mean, how is she?'

'She's feeling much better. I thought we could go and visit her this afternoon.'

'But aren't we meeting up for coffee?'

He paused. 'Sure . . . I guess so.'

'What I mean is, we shouldn't just drop in on her,' I backpedalled. 'Girls don't like that. Give her time to fix herself up.'

'Lucky I got you keeping me in line. You're a cool girl.'

After he hung up, I paced up and down my room, giving the torn-up floorboards a wide berth. I knew I should check my drawers and sweep under my bed to make sure the hungry ghost hadn't left anything else behind.

But all I could think of was Dean leaning back on his gaming chair, freshly showered, a drop of water clinging to his jawline as if it couldn't bear to leave him.

What was wrong with me?

I reached into the top drawer of my bedside table and pulled out a $25 million Powerball lottery ticket. Grandma Wu had died when the ship she was on board was caught in a typhoon. Apparently, she'd been trying to flee to Taiwan to escape gambling debts. It seemed she made a lot of bad choices in life. Then again, at least she'd taken risks.

This time, Grandma Wu was playing mah-jong with Uncle Hong Zi and two other ghosts when she appeared. One crone stared at me with eyes that blinked out of sync. She sipped a cup of steaming tea, which streamed straight out again through a hole in her neck. The second ghost peeked at me from behind a curtain of hair. From a certain angle, her oval face looked perfectly beautiful and demure. Without warning, she pushed back her chair and scampered towards me, her long fingernails scraping across the floor, leaving familiar scratch marks.

My blood ran cold. This must have been the ghost that had been creeping around my room. As she advanced, her hair parted, revealing round eyes and no mouth.

I screamed and backed into the wall. Uncle Hong Zi laughed.

Grandma Wu yanked her back by her hair. 'Jui Jui isn't happy with you. You don't keep much food around your room, do you?'

'I left fruit in the fruit bowl,' I protested.

She settled Jui Jui back into her seat and lit up a cigarette. 'So you're back again, little swift. And with a brightness to your eyes, a clearness in your complexion, a little *qi* in your breath.'

'Grandma Wu, my friend Carrie is in hospital with gastro.' I tried to keep my tone light and conversational.

'Yes, I heard. Not to worry. Tummy bugs usually only last seventy-two hours.'

'Do you think Carrie picked up a bug that lasts longer?'

'That depends.' She picked up the fortune tile from the discard pile and made a matching triplet with the tiles in her hand.

'The thing is, Grandma . . .' I skirted around the mahjong table and picked up the pot of tea. Carefully, I filled up her cup. 'Things have been going well for me lately. I'm acing my exams, I'm head of orchestra and there's this boy I like . . . I just worry that Carrie coming back might mess things up for me.'

Grandma Wu patted my hand. 'You're a good girl . . . but you're going to have to do a lot better than this if you want any more favours.'

'What?'

'Little swift, I'm your grandmother, not your bloody fairy godmother.' She drew the lottery ticket out of her pocket and waved it around. 'If you want my help, cough up. I want a first-division lottery ticket, every week. Get Jui Jui something tasty or she'll leave more than rice pellets in your room.'

'She doesn't even have a mouth!'

Jui Jui growled and lunged for me like a feral animal.

'And Daiyu wants a mobile phone with limitless data.' Grandma jabbed her finger at the ghost with the hole in her neck.

I was backed into the corner, on the verge of tears. 'How am I meant to bring her a mobile phone?' My voice came out paper-thin and whispery. Even ghosts had more substance than me.

Uncle Hong Zi shook his head, the two fans on either side of his scholar cap flapping. 'You can buy cardboard smartphone replicas from AliExpress, stupid girl. And I want you to get me—'

'Hush! Don't make her cry.' Grandma Wu ran her fingers through my hair. 'You'll never be the brightest, Christina, but there's hope for you yet.'

The Clarence Children's Centre had a two-hour visiting window. Dean was sitting by Carrie's bed when I arrived. I'd practised smiling on the train and my cheek muscles felt overstretched. I wished Dean had waited for me like I'd asked him to, so we could arrive together. That way, I wouldn't have had to walk in while Carrie was stroking his jaw.

Being sick didn't make Carrie less attractive. Her waxy skin and hollowed eyes gave her an ethereal beauty. 'Christina, you look great! Did you do something to your hair?'

'I put in some streaks last night.'

'Doesn't it look great?' Carrie asked Dean.

'Sure does,' he said, without looking up. 'So do you.'

'Awww.'

They mushed their mouths together again. Look at them. Just golden.

Carrie seemed to be eating just fine, no signs of a stomach virus. A half-eaten meat pie sat on her lunch tray, a smear of gravy and mashed potatoes left on the plate beside it. She'd even eaten the tri-coloured jelly dessert.

It was my gut that was churning. This was so unfair. I'd done everything Grandma Wu asked: I'd withdrawn my savings to buy more lottery tickets and the joss-cardboard phone. I even bought a cardboard modem, because who knew how data worked in the hell realms.

'I love you, babe.' Carrie looked up at Dean, a pretty blush on her pale visage.

A cicada scuttled across the linoleum floor and disappeared underneath the bed.

'When are they going to discharge you?' Dean leaned over and nuzzled her ear.

'Stop!' she giggled.

Definitely time to go. I slid my backpack from my shoulder and crouched down to rummage for Carrie's schoolwork. Maybe Dean could help her with the biology homework. We were doing sex-ed for the hundredth time. They rammed that stuff home in Catholic schools.

I set the books onto the hospital tray with a thump and accidentally squashed a cicada. I looked up. Dean and Carrie were still carrying on. They didn't notice the cicadas crawling out of the half-eaten meat pie, sticky with tomato sauce.

For a second, I thought it was a hallucination, before sandalwood singed my nostrils.

Uncle Hong Zi . . .

The cicadas' chirps escalated.

When he finally showed up, I was drifting in that space between sleep and wake. One moment I was in bed and the next, I found myself at the family shrine, putting out the incense. When I turned around, he was sitting in Mum's old rocking chair.

'Where's Grandma Wu?' I asked.

'Meddlesome old woman. Let's not talk about her.' Uncle Hong Zi curled a finger around a long, dangling whisker. He looked like a catfish.

'Why is Dean still with her?' I asked bluntly.

'Maybe you didn't want it enough.'

'But I do want it!' I practically stamped my foot.

'What do you want exactly?'

'I want to be with Dean! I want to lead the orchestra. I want to come first in maths – no, I want to top the whole grade!' My voice rose to a high-pitched whine. I itched to punch the walls, smash the statue of Guan Gong, hurl the peaches at Uncle Hong Zi and his smug face. It was unbearable having him see me undone. Raving. Ranting. Wanting.

'I can give you all that.' Uncle Hong Zi waved his hand, a magician reassuring his audience that he concealed nothing. 'I only ask for one thing in return.'

I needed fresh air. The sickly sweetness from the incense

filled my head, and the smoke stung my eyes. Rituals were about performing set actions in a prescribed order.

Repeat something enough and the weight of the action ceased to have meaning.

You scratch my back, I scratch yours. Judging by the way Uncle was clawing at his collar – the folds of skin on his neck, raw and red – he wanted something badly.

He walked up the stairs, pausing to wait for me on the landing. I swallowed hard. Curiosity won, and I followed him past my parents' door, past Michelle's door and into my bedroom. The smell of sandalwood was overwhelming. He paused to look at the pin-up board hanging on the wall over my desk. Along with post-it reminders, postcards and badges, there was a photo of the senior orchestra from the music festival last year. Instead of in height order, Mr Minchin had arranged us in our sections. Because I was so short, half my face was cut off by Carrie's head.

Uncle Hong Zi fingered the picture of Carrie. Her flaxen hair scrunched up in a high ponytail, her bright eyes, apple cheeks. Without warning, he tore the photo from the tack. 'Give her to me.'

I picked up the scissors and cut out the Carrie silhouette. My hand was shaking.

'Careful, girlie.'

When I was done, we headed back to the altar room. The candlestick lamps cast an eerie red glow over Uncle's face. He pawed at his neck like a dog scratching at fleas.

Before I could change my mind, I placed the photo fragment into the incense burner and grabbed the lighter. Uncle Hong Zi didn't bother hiding the naked hunger on his face. He licked his lips in time with the flames licking Carrie's photo.

Tinder. That was all she amounted to. And I was the flame that needed to keep burning. Once Uncle's hunger was fed, mine would be too. I watched as the heat took every part of her: the hair, the long legs covered in sheer stockings, the black-patent heels.

She brought this on herself.

She should have known better than to eat the apple.

Do I See It All Now?

MICHELLE O'CONNELL

My story is inspired by growing up being neurodivergent and undiagnosed.

A girl experiences life through her own lens. Her understanding of the world and how she is treated is filtered through it, perceiving negative and dangerous situations as neutral and harmless until later.

While growing up, she sees glimpses of reality. Every life event cracks the lens she sees the world through, until she eventually sees it for how it really is.

Do I See It All Now?

Angel Eyes

ALISON EVANS

The angels arrived to cleanse the sins of the wolves. That's what the posters say anyway, but I haven't seen anything yet so maybe I'm taking it too literally. As I shift back, my snout turns into a nose, my teeth shrink, my hands lengthen, my skin comes back. Standing on two legs, I wipe the rabbit blood from my mouth and spit out a little bone.

'It's getting light. Someone will see it's us.'

Only the slightest hint of dawn is appearing, but we gotta be careful cause if we get caught, shit'll really hit the fan. Dunno if the others have seen the posters yet.

Tom growls at me, teeth bared. They're the last bit of the wolf that remains till he's all the way human again. 'Always gotta be right, Zero.'

I grin at him. 'Yep.'

'We crash at yours?'

He's not really asking. Since school holidays started, every night we go out to hunt he stays at mine. We sleep like the wolves we are, in a warm pile of sweat and breath, no blankets.

We walk through the chest-high, prickly weeds to get to the bike path. Behind us, a freight train roars past, loud as anything. As we get to the road, the only sound near is the beep-beep of the crossing button and we just cross anyway; there's no cars. Station car park's almost empty and we start to walk to my place.

The closest train track's about a metre from our back fence. When we first moved in after Grandad died, the noise'd keep me up at night, but now I like it. The rhythm of the trains, the way they remind me that there's always someone out there, going someplace.

Tom stops dead in his tracks halfway to my house, nose darkening as he starts to shift. 'Can you smell that?' His teeth forming spikes in his mouth before he finishes the sentence.

'Wait—' I say, but he's fully shifted and running on all fours. I start to race after him, spine melting and reforming, snout jutting out, bitumen scratchy under the soft pads of my feet. I growl as I chase him, but as soon as I get a whiff of what Tom's chasing, my mouth waters and I imagine tearing into it, blood dripping down my chin. Fox.

It's been ages since we had any fox, that's why we've been feeding on rabbits for so long. Tom takes the lead and I nip at his heels as the disappearing night sings around us. I follow him to an access lane running between some houses. This one's got a ditch in the middle that's collected leaves and shit for a hundred years in between the uneven cobblestones.

I stop to sniff at the edge of a roller door, then I see Tom: frozen, hackles up.

When I look to see what he's looking at, I whine in pain. Something too bright, *too much too much*. Can't look at it properly, but I growl, same as Tom.

Whatever it is starts to come down the alleyway towards us, and there's a tug, a vacuum, something telling me to get nearer. I dig my paws in, snarling. The light gets closer and when I start to see it properly, my eyes burn. Like looking at the sun, but I can't look away.

Light, eyes, an endless wheel: spinning and furious and devastating. As I look, blotches appear across my vision and fear thrills through me, rippling my skin, turning my stomach.

In my head, I hear the being: *All things must end.* Their voice like nothing I've heard before. Like knees across gravel, skin peeling, blood spotting.

Patches of heat appear on my chest, my mouth tastes like metal and I wonder what the posters meant – to cleanse our sins.

Tom crashes right into me, slamming us both into the ground. The angel's spell is broken, and we scamper back down the alley, away from their terrible light. After a couple of streets running, we can't see the light following us, so we stop.

Tom starts to whine softly, but I can barely hear it cause I'm trying not to spew. I lick his face once, then take off home. He follows and soon we're running side by side.

When we climb in through my window, we're barely human again and the house is shaking from a passing train. Don't bother with showering or nothing, just curl up on my bed. We don't speak as we listen to the thunder of the train.

'That was one of them, wasn't it?' I whisper, though I know

the answer, my head in the crook of one of his elbows. His sweat is fresh.

Tom squeezes his eyes shut. 'It hurt to look at it, Zero.'

'Yeah.'

He swallows, his hand squeezing mine.

Next morning, Tom's gone. I feel his absence too sharp and I lie there like there's no one else left in the whole world, staring at where he should be. I shiver, thinking back to the angel. I can feel the tug in my chest, my ribs still. Like something was taken. My mouth tastes like metal and I can still smell the burning.

When I strip off to shower, there's a red, itchy lump on my chest. I scratch it, but it's tender and I wince. After I wash last night's sweat off, I slather some cream on the lump, but it doesn't seem to do anything. I brush my teeth, but I can still taste the metal. My eyes have big purple bruises underneath them.

Tom's left the testosterone next to the sink. He's over often enough that we just share, and he'll bring one of his bottles when it needs replacing. I rub it into my thigh and get dressed.

When I go to the kitchen to get brekky, Mum's bag is on the table. She's working nights at the moment so she must already be in bed.

I take my cereal bowl outside and sit looking out at the field, its grass all yellow and crunchy. The air stinks like cat litter and dead things – either the meatworks, or the tallow place is going off again.

A train goes past, the blue Sydney one. It runs on the track closest to the house, and leaves at about 7 am. Another one comes in at 7 pm.

I swallow, try to ignore the vacuum, try to dislodge it with a cough, but it won't go away. I scratch the lump but wince again at the pain.

When twilight begins, I tell Mum I'm going for a walk. She's getting ready for her shift at the hospital, and so she nods, tells me to eat something good for dinner and leaves me some cash. I don't tell her it'll probably be some pest animal and I won't be back for hours cause I'll be hunting with the others. After Tom had a go at us for eating anything that moved, we only eat the introduced species: mostly rabbit, mynas and mice. Fox, if we're lucky.

Sometimes I feel like I should tell Mum about being a wolf, but it's nice having something that only a few people know about. The pack is my secret.

I cross the road as soon as I walk out our gate and though I don't mean to, I find myself back at the access lane where we saw the angel. A quick detour before I meet the others in Footscray.

It's empty except for the rubbish. I never seen anyone else in one of these, everyone always uses the footpaths and the roads, not the back alleys. The angel's the first anything I seen here that wasn't an animal.

Walking slow, careful, I shift into the wolf: my bones shift and grate, the muscles shift around them, harden and grow taut. Keeping my nose to the ground, I smell the heat and the ire from last night and the closer I get to the spot we saw them, the stronger the tug in my ribs gets.

That's all. All that's left are smells and the vacuum.

The vacuum throbs now, in time with my heart, and my paws are rooted to the spot. I breathe in slow, try not to let the whine escape from round my teeth, but it does, low and soft.

I can feel eyes on me.

There's a rustling to the right, and though I can smell it's only a possum, my hackles raise. The possum gets to the top of the closest fence before running away.

The burning smell remains. Faint, but it's there.

The vacuum pulses and I cough, switching back to human form all at once, dizzy from the sudden height. My skin is still crawling and the hairs on my arms are raised, but at least I can't smell the burning as sharply.

The lump on my chest spikes in itchiness and I reach to scratch it, then yelp. I peer down my shirt and my vision folds in on itself. I sway, hear the blood in my ears.

There's an eye growing on my skin.

Not human, not wolf. I stare at it and want to vomit again, but I just piss-bolt out of the access lane and towards the station, getting Tom's number up so I can call him. It rings out. My palms sweat and I make sure to grip my phone extra tight as I call him again.

'Call me as soon as you can,' I say into his message bank.

The train's packed but it's only a couple of minutes to Footscray anyway. When we pull into Footscray station, I pause before stepping onto the platform. Something's changed; the air is different. Can't tell any more without transforming.

I get on the escalator. At the top, a jolt runs through me. There's an eye, staring. It's the same poster as we've seen before, the ones that say *to cleanse the sins of the wolves*, but the eye is a new addition. It's on every poster.

A shiver runs up my spine as I stare into the eye. I reach up a hand, press my palm over it. My palm starts to burn; I wince but hesitate before pulling away.

Flick's house is near the Maribyrnong, so we meet down near the riverbank under the bridge. Tom's not there yet, but Flick and Salima are sitting on one of the concrete pillars. Salima gives a wave.

'So they're real,' Flick says when I'm close enough. 'You alright?' They pull me into a hug, crushing me to their chest.

When I'm released, I shake my head. 'No. Look at this.' I pull my shirt collar down and watch their faces turn from curious to horrified.

Salima covers her mouth with a hand. 'That matches—' She pulls a crumpled piece of paper out of the pocket of her long skirt. It's the same poster I saw at the station.

Flick reads off the paper. 'That's not good.'

'Someone was handing them out in Sunshine.' Salima shakes her head. 'I mean, I knew people knew about us, but I didn't think we'd be uh . . .'

'Sinners?' Flick says.

'Hellooo, yes?' Tom says from behind me, but his smile slips when he sees none of us are laughing. 'What?'

Salima hands him the flyer.

'And this,' I say, showing him my chest.

He stares wordlessly, as he turns and lifts the back of his shirt. Just to the right of his spine is an eye that perfectly matches the one on my body. I reach out, realise what I'm doing, put my hand down.

'Is that why you left?' I ask quietly.

He doesn't meet my gaze. 'Yeah.'

'What are we gonna do?' Salima asks Flick. 'Are we all gonna get eyes?'

'It feels itchy before it grows,' I say. 'I think it's cause we saw the angel.'

Flick's phone lights up in their hand and they frown. 'It's Gremlin.'

Flick always tells us to only call if it's an emergency – with their hearing aids it's hard for them to hear on the phone. It's way more accessible when they can see what the other person is saying.

'Hey hey, calm down, where are you?'

I can hear Gremlin's panicked voice. In response, my bones start to shake; they want to transform. After a few moments, Flick turns back to us. 'We have to go.'

Flick shifts into a wolf and we follow suit. Soon as I'm fully shifted, I smell the river, the joggers, and I realise Gremlin's not too far: down the river, near the wetlands. Means we'll have to run where people can see us, but sometimes we just have to.

This time of night, there aren't heaps of people out anyway, though we scare the shit out of a jogger with their headphones in. Flick out in front, Tom next to me and Salima guarding us at the back.

Flick howls as we run, and I join in, loud enough that they can hear. Our voices loop around each other as we bound along. A plane goes by overhead and I howl more, trying to drown it out. Together, it feels like we do.

The river glistens under the moon as we pass the temple and Mazu, run under the bridge covered in bird shit, get to the wetlands. We jump the gate and as we run up the hill, I see a glow not too far away. Tom pants next to me, his breath hot.

Gremlin yelps and my nose shrivels from the smell as we get closer.

When we get there, a different angel is looming over Gremlin. This one is made of wings: layers and layers of wings breathing over each other, whispering seeping from them like snake tongues.

Gremlin's whining, but when she sees us, her ears prick up. The Wings turns for a moment, and Gremlin gets a swipe in. The Wings screeches and bats Gremlin into the ground.

For a moment, I want to run. But I see Gremlin there, trapped just like me and Tom were last night, and she's all alone. I don't wait for direction from Flick, just rush past them and clamp my teeth down on the tip of the closest wing. The Wings screeches again as they turn to me, and heavy feathers try to bat me away. I growl through my teeth as I stay locked on, trying to stay fierce though my eyes and nose are burning.

Something lifts me up by the ankle from behind. My leg feels like it's being ripped from its socket, and I twist in the air to see a new angel. Wings cover their feet and face, but as they draw me closer, I see their face is nothing but eyes.

As The Eyes dangles me in the air, I see the angel from the first night not too far behind. They're rounding us up.

Flick snarls, jaws snapping as they try to get to me, and Salima and Tom join in.

Repent, The Eyes sounds in my head.

My leg socket screams, and patches of itchy heat travel up my leg. The Eyes is ripping from me my strong bones, my teeth, my hunger for meat, my bond with the others. My limbs lengthen and my fur starts to disappear. My teeth shrink small and I can't smell anything.

Gremlin rips a chunk off The Wings and The Eyes screeches at the same time; I clap my hands over my ears but the shriek pierces too deep. The Eyes drops me and I land in pain. The Eyes spreads its wings over Gremlin, bathing everything in a horrible light, and I have to look away as Gremlin's wolf is taken away. I feel Gremlin's loss in me, deep and pooling inside my ribcage.

A warning, the angels chorus. *All things must end.*

They glow brighter and brighter; I close my eyes and when I open them again, the angels are gone, leaving the burning smell behind once more.

'Gremlin?' I say, but I can't move without fire racing up my leg. There are red lumps around my ankle where the Eyes grabbed me, and they peter out up my leg. Some are already growing eyelashes. I look away, my stomach turning.

The others rush to her, in a mish-mash of wolf and human bodies. Flick is the first to fully transform back into human and they crouch beside Gremlin who is covered in red lumps too.

'I'm not hurt,' Gremlin says. 'But my wolf is gone.'

We're silent as a train goes by.

Tom touches my hand. 'Are you okay?'

'My leg,' I say, though it's nothing compared to Gremlin. 'Gremlin . . .'

'Don't,' she says. 'You would do the same.'

Salima starts to feel my leg, testing the range of movement, asking me if certain positions hurt. She takes care not to touch the eyes. 'I think you should be okay,' she says. 'But we should rest for a while.'

'Why didn't they take it from all of us?' Tom asks.

Flick shakes their head. 'I don't know.'

'Do you reckon that'll happen to us?' I ask as we watch Flick running back home on all fours.

Tom shakes his head. 'I don't wanna think about it.'

A train goes past, horn blaring, but neither of us flinch. We watch it thunder down the tracks, its light pooling onto us. The cicadas start up again once the train's gone.

Tom sits and I lie beside him, flat-out on the cool ground. The lumps on my legs are mostly eyes now. I watch them blink under the lightening sky.

'How can they do that?' Tom asks. He lies down, looking at the sky instead of me. His arm rests against mine and neither of us move.

I look at Tom. It's different to sleeping tangled in the same bed, lying like this. Out in the open. It's so close; too close. Tom looks at me. Cicadas.

A plane flies low overhead, so loud that I don't have to answer him.

Tom pulls my forehead to his. We stay there, breathing each other's air as a freight train rumbles past for what feels like hours.

A new poster crops up in the Tottenham underpass a week later: *A warning to the wolves. Repent. You will be saved.* These ones have more eyes on them: multiplying, crowding the page.

I tear it down, but as I walk further, I see another. My jaw elongates and I snarl, tear the next poster down too. I shake my head, my bones re-setting to human, and try to keep walking.

A train rumbles overhead – V/Line, it's not stopping – and a burning starts on the inside of my knee. I've been wearing pants or long skirts borrowed from Salima to cover the eyes, but I know they're there. Blinking and searching, rolling.

I get on the train to Sunshine, and Gremlin's house, and the whole ride there I'm itchy as anything, like I've got fleas. We haven't been hunting for a week now and I need it. It's getting darker – now's the time we'd be getting ready to go out.

I fidget in my seat, my hands shaking with the effort of staying human, close my eyes, shove my knuckles in my ears. Listen to my own blood.

The smell of the fish and chips wafts up as Gremlin unwraps the bundle of butcher's paper. My mouth waters. She starts tearing up the paper for plates. Tom comes back outside with vinegar and mayo, and Flick picks a lemon off the tree.

'Reckon we'll hunt this week?' Tom asks, as everyone starts grabbing food.

Flick shakes their head. 'I dunno. Too risky.'

'What, so we're just going to never be wolves again?' Tom balls his fists in his lap.

'We should still hunt,' I say, ripping off a piece of flake. 'Just not alone.' My eyes meet Tom's for a sec. He grins and looks away and I wish everyone would go home so we could be alone.

'We could just go for a run tonight,' Salima says. 'Gremlin, you could ride your bike? We can't let them stop us.'

Gremlin shakes her head. 'It's bad enough being stuck like this, I don't need a reminder.'

'It's too dangerous,' Flick says. 'We don't know enough about them.'

'So we're just gonna hide away?' Tom snarls, and his wolf-teeth come down. He pulls up his sleeves, exposing the eyes growing on his skin. 'Pretty hard to hide that.'

He gets up, walks off.

'Tom—' I follow him around the side of the house, where he sits on the side-door step, head in his hands.

'Why do they hate us?' he asks, gaze fixed on the ground. 'What's the difference anyway? They're just like us. It's not like we're monsters. We're just wolves.'

I sit next to him and pull up the skirt Salima lent me. 'They're kind of like pimples.'

Tom doesn't move.

'If pimples made me want to vomit '

I'd hoped that would get a smile, or at least get him to look at me.

'You wanna go home?' As I speak, his belly rumbles. 'Let's just eat, yeah?' He doesn't reply, and I stand up. 'Well, I'm gonna have something.'

'Wait, Zero,' he says. 'Sorry. I'm just . . . you go, I'll join yas in a sec.'

'Maybe the eyes will fade, inshallah,' Salima is saying as I come back. 'It's easy for me to hide them with the way I dress, but they're disgusting.'

'When we transform, the eyes disappear,' I say as I sit down. 'Did you notice?'

'I wonder what that means,' Flick says, and the others continue talking.

I try to eat, but I want the hunt. My hands shake with it. I watch the others try to smile as they chat, but it's all hollow. The sticky night-time heat of Gremlin's backyard is making me sweat. It drips down the backs of my knees.

Crouching down, I take a closer look at the eyes on my legs. Can the angels see through them?

I hover a finger over the highest eye on my leg, just under my knee. The iris follows the movements of my finger, and I move it closer and closer, until my fingertip is millimetres away from the wet surface.

Gently, I press my finger to the iris. I can't feel anything, but the eye blinks a few times. I tug at the eyelashes, and the eye rolls, but I only feel it where the eyelid is connected to the skin on my leg. It's like pieces of the angels are growing on me.

I rush over to the side of Gremlin's backyard and spew, though I've barely eaten since lunch so nothing really comes out. Fluid, mostly. I shudder, but my stomach keeps rolling. I get down on my knees, retching and spitting. At least I can taste something other than metal for the first time in a week.

'Zero?' Flick puts their hand on my back.

I wipe my mouth with the back of my hand. Flick's leaning down and so I can see down their shirt a little. Their chest is dotted with eyes. My stomach cramps.

'I'm gonna check on Tom.' I walk round the side of the house, but no one's there.

I shift into the wolf and immediately I can smell him, in wolf-form, running down the road. I yap to the others, still sitting round the table in their human forms, and take off. As I run, I howl, letting him know I'm coming, though I know he'll smell me.

He's off down the reserve next to the train tracks. The others will follow me.

I smell burning.

When I howl, Tom doesn't reply.

I find him by the tracks, human, staring at the rising moon. I shift back and pull him into a hug. When he hugs me back it feels like he'll never let go. Weight drops from my shoulders.

'Sorry Zero,' he says into my neck. 'I just needed to run.'

We break apart. 'Me too. Just like, tell me next time. It's dangerous right now.'

The hairs on the back of my neck stand up as I say it. Tom sees them first, and he points for me to turn around.

The Eyes is in front, the others behind. Tom's mouth is first to shift. He growls, white teeth shining in the angels' light. The rest of his body follows, and while I'm shifting, he rushes right for The Eyes.

The Wings swoops up and bats him down. He tries to get his teeth into the feathers as they whisper promises of salvation.

I smell Salima and Flick not too far off, so I let the wolf take me. Claws sprout and teeth jut out as I shrink and grow, and I run to join Tom.

The Eyes is closest, so I aim for them, growling as I run. They try to grab me but I roll away, digging my paws into the dirt before racing back at them, aiming for neck hidden beneath the wings. I dodge wings again and when I see their face covered in eyes – the same eyes that are all over me – I don't hesitate, though my stomach rolls.

I get my teeth around their neck, start to clamp down, but they grip each side of my jaw, prise me off them and drop me to the ground in a pile of bones and fur.

I whine, and they hit me with heavy wings. I close my eyes – they're too bright to look at for too long – and I smell that Flick and Salima are here.

Flick howls, but they're cut off.

I stand on all fours. There's an ache near the bottom of my ribs and I can barely open my eyes. My mouth tastes like metal and blood. The Eyes towers above, and behind them I can see Salima and Flick in human form. Did the Wheel take their wolves away?

'Zero!' Tom calls to me. 'Let's just go.'

I start to back away from the Eyes in all their glory, horrifying and magnificent.

Creatures such as you should heed warnings, The Eyes says before batting me again with their heavy wings.

My snout hits the ground and I whine, the Eyes glows brighter, my bones shrink, the bulk of me disappears; my human skin breaks as my nose scrapes against the gravel.

As The Eyes moves closer, I scrabble backwards, my fingers fumbling for broken glass or stones. A weapon, something, anything. But there's nothing, not even a twig to poke in an eye.

As I stare into the vacuum of eyes covering their body, my fears are sucked up into my mouth. Never seeing Tom again, never running with the others, facing the endless void after death.

All things must end, on a loop in my head. Its terrible voice. I'm just a speck under a shoe, a creature being run over by a car. *All things must end.*

But no, Tom was right. We don't have any sin: no more than angels or anyone else.

I glance over at Tom, The Wings hovering over him, and Salima and Flick cornered by The Wheel. The last of my anger blooms. I pull down the collar of my shirt and show The Eyes my chest.

'Look at yourself,' I tell them, words choked out around the vacuum.

The Eyes falters.

I push myself up off the ground. My head spins, but I make my legs carry the weight of me again. 'Look!'

The eyes on my legs start to burn. Each one trained on the angel. The vacuum pulls stronger, and I'm drawn towards it. The Eyes tries to pull away from me, but it's drawn to me too, by a force like a magnet. A low keen sounds out, and I realise it must be coming from them. Layers and layers of sounds start to fold in over themselves, and my ears sting but I can't cover them.

I close my own eyes as the eyes on my skin burn hotter. I grit my teeth, taste blood in my mouth. The cuts and scrapes on my fingers sing out, and I feel blood pouring from them. Too much for such little scrapes.

I sway on my feet, but the vacuum keeps me upright. Something forces my eyes open and I see The Eye extending a hand towards me. I grip it, feeling how cold and unforgiving their flesh is.

Why are you doing this? The Eyes asks me.

'I'm not,' I say. I pull my shirt off, so that all the eyes on my chest are exposed. 'You are.'

The sounds reach a cacophony and blinding light pours out of The Eyes. They drop me and as they disappear behind bright light, my skin blisters and pops before I can shield my face. I crouch on the ground, eyes tight shut, and listen to the agonising end of the angels.

The eyes on my body burn themselves clean off, and when the light finally dies down, my arms and chest are smooth again.

When I open my eyes, there's a person crumpled where The Eyes was standing. We're the same age. They're staring, not moving, but I can see them breathing.

'Zero?' Tom brushes my elbow and I jump.

'Sorry.'

The teen in front of me sits up. They're shaking.

'Are you okay?' I ask them, though I don't move closer or try to touch them.

Our eyes meet and I feel something pass between us: a shiver. They see who they are.

'Let's just go,' Flick says. They pull my arm, and I let them lead me away.

We start off down the railway tracks, slow from all our injuries. The moon shines off the metal and I can feel the rumble of a train coming, so we move to the side. As it passes, I think I hear a howl split through the roar of the train.

I spin around, looking for where it came from.

Gremlin is running behind the train, tongue lolling from the side of her mouth. As wolves, we come together. Tom licks my face, Gremlin's tail wags fast as anything. We howl and we run, even though it hurts.

Best Years of Your Life

FELIX WILKINS

Here's a hot take fuelled by angst, hormones and experience: I fucking hate Australia.

I hate the fact that ninety-nine percent of us wouldn't be here if a wave of evil bastards hadn't murdered, pillaged, raped and stolen. I hate the way we casually dismiss problems with a grumbled, *she'll be right*. I hate the way we've always perceived the USA as being all backwards and weird, but a majority of the music, television, food, art, movies, books and culture that Australians consume come directly from America.

I hate the way we simultaneously love and hate authority, so they cancel each other out and we almost never protest anything, and nothing ever changes as a result. I hate that we're so geographically isolated from the rest of the world, and how that has the side-effect of turning an online purchase of a twenty-dollar aroma diffuser into a ninety-dollar shipping fee. I hate the way that certain suburbs have custom-built, three-storey houses with 'fuck you' balcony views just a few doors down from dilapidated public housing units. I hate the way my mum and everyone above forty has an inexplicable nostalgia for Cold Chisel and Kylie Minogue. I hated the look on my dad's face last Sunday when *Gallipoli* came on Channel Nine and he raised his Carlton Dry and went 'Mel Gibson? Australian hero'.

I hate that the country itself is geared towards a specific subset of upper-class white men, and anyone less wealthy or privileged is essentially a second-class citizen. I hate that I see no future for myself as everything gets more expensive and existing homeowners continue to feast upon the housing market and unemployment rates get higher and higher.

I hate that vocalising most of this to anyone results in a disapproving look, as if to say, 'Well *I'm* happy, so you don't know what you're talking about'.

A cocktail of stress, overdue assignments, and literal cocktails by way of Mum's liquor cabinet had me waking sporadically last night, each time angrier with myself and the world than the last. It's almost 1 am, and I'm probably about to begin the cycle again any minute now. I'd chuck on some Netflix but it feels like I've already seen everything worth seeing – and definitely my fair share of things not worth seeing.

Is this how it feels to have peaked at seventeen? Usually people who peak at this age at least have their looks to carry them through hardship, so with every fibre of my six-foot-one being, I bloody well hope not. I wonder how Passiona and red wine taste when you mix them together. Maybe I should go make nachos – I've got some vegetarian chilli I could defrost. I could take a bath to warm myself up – I've had the heating on in my room all night, and I'm still freezing my tits off. I keep running through scenarios, thinking of things to do to distract myself or help me get to sleep, but I can't bring myself to actually *do* any of it.

I'm ashamed to admit that I keep thinking about my day at school. No matter how many times I remind myself that I can't control other people, and that it ultimately doesn't matter, I can't help but think about every moment that seemed wrong. Every time a guy looked up to talk to me and I could tell they felt weird doing so. Friends saying one thing but meaning something else. Year Ten kids gawking at my unshaven legs. Teachers deciding it was easier to brush off a question than engage with it. My brain works overtime on locating and analysing problems that may or may not exist. How great would it be if someone were to sit you down on your eleventh birthday and gently teach you how to do it.

How to not feel everything all the time.

What time is it? Shit. *Bathroom.* Get to the bathroom, now. Oh, nice. Good going Tori; pale yellow bile and chunks of last night's curry now adorn your tiles. Better go get a bucket and Ajax Spray & Wipe. And it's not even 6 am yet. Bloody hate munting. The way my whole upper torso just lurches forward and I can't control my own body, like some sadistic puppeteer's pulling at my stomach. How I involuntarily drop to my knees and cling to the foul-smelling sides of the toilet bowl for desperately needed support. I try to remember to tie back my hair, but it's always too late. Spicy stomach acid coats the back of my throat and clings to my teeth – I need something to wash it down.

Hold on . . . in the centre of the vomit pool. That doesn't look like curry. What the fuck is that? Did I just cough up a kidney stone? Can't have – there's more than one. I think they're literal stones. Yeah, there must be six or seven little rocks.

Jesus Christ, I'm going to be sick again.

I don't even want to look at Mum or Dad this morning. I hate how people brush you off when you try to vent about your parents annoying you: *no shit Tori, all parents are annoying.* Like somehow that's supposed to make them more tolerable?

Dad's probably still asleep, so if I can just avoid having a full conversation with Mum, I'll be right. Shit, she's in the kitchen – that's fine, it's fine, I can just grab a cup of coffee, an apple, my jersey, and head out the door. 'Busy one at school today, darl?' I can never dignify that with a response. Just grunt back at her. *Fuck*, that was unnecessarily loud. I hope she doesn't try to play the *watch your tone* card with me this morning.

Is my jersey somehow growing in the wash, or are my arms getting shorter? I'm sure all the lovely ladies and germs at school will find that so alluring – a ten-foot-tall girl with arms the size of Milky Ways. Thankfully, Mum seems to have taken the hint from my not-so-subtle grunt, and she's acting as if I've already left the house. Christ, why is her being silent worse than her not shutting up? Is she trying to make me feel bad? Whatever, I'm not dealing with that this morning, especially not over a *slightly* abnormal grunt.

The school canteen's especially crap today. Maybe I could have opted for the pasta instead of the veggie Chiko roll. So cold out. Why didn't I take a jacket to school? What's the weather, anyway? Ha, twenty-four degrees, my arse. Wouldn't need a jacket if the Year 12 jerseys weren't so thin. Cheapskates. I can see the veins underneath my hands turning blue-ish black – Jesus, it looks like my skin is too. Time to invest in a pair of gloves?

Oh shit, I thought Rebecca didn't notice me come in this morning. Well, she clearly knows I'm here now. Should I tell her I have cramps? It's technically not a lie, but she's just going to offer me a Nurofen. Stomach bug?

I don't even know why I'm trying to get her to leave me alone right now. Usually she'd be great at helping me feel better. I just don't feel like being around anyone right now. She looks disappointed. God, I hate that face. She doesn't even have to say anything. She thinks eleven years of friendship mean she knows what I need better than I do. I just want to reach over and dig my nails into the skin by her cheekbone, then rip back my hand as fast as possible and watch that stupid fucking judgemental face come with it. If you're just going to stand there silently, I won't say anything either. *Come on.* Take the hint and move on, already. The silent treatment doesn't give you the moral high ground: it just makes you a petty, immature child.

Come on. Leave me. Leave. Leave me. Leave me now.

Leave me now, Rebecca.

Leave me now.

Leave me now.

Leave me.

Even after the shower, my hair hurts like crazy when I brush it. It's unruly, weirdly thick and tough to the touch. Almost feels like a tangle of wires and cables emanating from my scalp. Maybe I've gone too long without a wash. This is always the worst part of getting out of the shower, or being in the bathroom in general – being in front of a mirror. Right here and now is the optimal time to notice things you don't like about yourself, like a crooked tooth, or your weirdly shaped hips, or the way your eyes look when you smile, or how matted and gross your hair is.

Usually I have an aversion to shaving body hair. The constant itchiness from the regrowth is bad enough as it is, but I hate the idea that somehow it's disgusting for women to not shave their armpits, whereas men can look like Cousin It from the waist down and it's supposed to be chill. However, for whatever reason, my leg hair is *much* thicker than it usually is, and it's all knotted together. I imagine confessing to a guy that I have thick leg hair. Watching as the cogs turn in his head as he pictures a single strand of hair, the height of a five o'clock shadow and as thick as a piece of thread. A tiny flaw. This is decidedly not that.

My leg hair is currently structurally similar to a rosemary plant: tiny little hairs growing on either side of longer hairs; like branches growing out of a trunk or stalks growing from a stem. There are layers upon layers of these strange little hairs. The tips are rough to the touch, yet light, like the worn bristles of an old paintbrush. Today may be the day that I finally break and shave my leg hair. It's not like they're usually picturesque, but I don't usually have quite so much of them. Ah, nothing like a mirror to stir up a little bit of overanalysis.

I shouldn't have to practically shove Dad out of my way the second I get home from school, but apparently that's just my home life.

'Why did you skip English?'

I'm just two steps into my house, where I'm supposed to come for shelter and a much-needed reprieve from another crap day. Mum's on my case too, as I can tell from the rapid knocking and the equally helpful, *come out, we need to have a talk* outside my bedroom door.

Do they get off on this? She must have been knocking for five minutes now. A normal person would have given up or respectfully given me some space after twenty seconds, but she's ready to blow her top. Her steaming anger doesn't subside or cool off: it just simmers, waiting for the moment when it can come bubbling out all at once. And then finally, after she's scalded everyone in the immediate vicinity, she'll be fine.

Now my itch is even worse – dammit, why can't I get that spot? My door threatens to cave in. Dad must be in the other room, sinking into his armchair as he listens to the screaming and knocking coming from outside my door. I can hear him turning up the volume on the footy. *Fuck, is she actually getting louder?* And bringing Rebecca into this? *Just stop.* She can't even take a moment to try to think about what might be going on on my side of the door. *Oh yes, refer to me by my government name, Victoria.* Very original. If she doesn't shut up . . .

Argh, that spot, just above the centre of my back, just barely out of reach. Does she want me to lose it at her? Is her aim to get me to listen? Because as I walk toward my bedroom door,

I'm not thinking about turning the lock and inviting her to continue the torrent of shouting within the comfort of my room. I'm thinking about charging at her head-first, knocking her to the floor, and stomping the ground next to her head. I want to watch her crawl and writhe around, telling me she was wrong, begging me to stop as my heel gets closer and closer to hitting her right in the centre of her neck. To watch her lower her fist and drop, rolling around on the carpet as I thrash wildly above her, and Dad heroically turns the footy up even louder to drown out the sound of his wife's screams.

I want to see her eyes in that moment, the light behind them growing dim as she gives up. I want to see the moment she realises she knocked one too many times. The moment she regrets pushing and pulling me all at once. The moment she realises she can't control me anymore. Because she can't.

That just came out of me. The booming echo of a voice, barely recognisable as my own, bounces off my walls and reverberates inside my skull. It sounded like my awkward grunt from the other morning, but stronger, deeper, more guttural – I didn't even realise I was speaking until I heard the echo. I can feel the floorboards beneath me rumbling, my books and records shaking in place on their shelves.

Jesus, that just came out of me?

The knocking has come to a complete standstill, and a long, satisfying tingle runs under my skin and through my veins, starting in the back of my neck and ending at the tips of my toes. I'm curling them without even meaning to. The tingle feels so overwhelmingly good. The silence on the other side of the door makes the feeling last longer, makes it even better. I almost need to sit down. The itch in my back went away for a second in all the excitement, but it's starting to return again, and worse.

Feels like I've got it. I'm digging underneath my shirt and into my back with a blunt pair of craft scissors, unwittingly provided by the under-stocked art supplies closet. I can feel the itch beginning to wear off as I push the edge of the scissors into the area between my shoulder blades. A little Year Seven boy passes the window, eyes wide as he looks at me sticking my arm up the back of my jumper. Presumably he's on his way to the library to play iPhone games with his friends or something. Feels like hot water's dripping down my back. The itch fades just a little bit every time I feel the scissor blade push into my flesh, so I'd better push harder. I hear repulsed noises coming from the hall behind me, so I prod the sharpest edge into the itchy spot extra hard, and immediately feel better, the sounds of judgement giving way to that increasingly familiar tingle.

Oh, is that Rebecca? Shit, we just made eye contact – I think she's walking towards me. She looks like she hasn't been sleeping well. I jab myself with the edge of the blade one last time, the hot liquid dripping down my back faster, before I drop the scissors and look up at her. *Let's just let her talk at us.*

Wow, she *really* hasn't been sleeping well. It's hard for me to listen with all the tingling, but I can hear that she's not herself. Something about *worried*. Something about *your parents*. Something about *can't do this*. What's she saying? Look into her eyes. She looks sad. I hear the words *I want to help* somewhere in there.

How long has she been talking to me? God, that spot is starting to itch worse than ever. The hot liquid grows hotter, almost scalding hot. It's getting harder to concentrate. Rebecca looks at me so plainly, so matter-of-fact – the sadness in her face is gone, and it's now as if she's looking right through me, like I'm not here. Is she done? Did she just say something? What?

'I think you need some time alone, Tori.'

Rebecca gave me exactly what I wanted.

Need another glass of water.

I'd thank her but I don't have anything to say to her.

I've wanted her to take the hint, to step off, for months – no, years even. Since we first became friends in Year One, she was always the one pushing the friendship along.

Need more water.

We'd always hang out with her friends. I'd go to Blockbuster with her on her way to her house every day after school even though I wanted to go to the newsagent, and we'd go to the Melbourne Show and White Night and Moomba with her parents and her brother. We'd go down to stay with her grandparents on the school holidays, and we'd teach other swear words that we heard from my dad or her brother (who's twelve years older, and from her mum's previous marriage).

Need more water.

She'd always push me to try weird foods with her and to swim in the deeper parts of the beach that my parents wouldn't let me swim in. She'd get me to help her throw rocks at boys who bullied us in Year Five, and when one of the boys slipped and cracked his head, she told the boy's parents she had done it alone and she got suspended from school for three days.

I don't need that level of control in my life, especially not right now.

Need another glass of water.

Back in front of the mirror. My itch feels better after dousing it in freezing water, but the rest of my body is cursing me for having a twenty-minute-long cold shower. I was weirdly hoping that my period arriving would help my mood a little bit, or at least give me some closure or perspective – *Hey Tori, I know you've been feeling like your last marble just went down the marble run, but that's normal! It's just hormones!*

But the more I've thought about it, the more I realise I've felt crazy for longer than the last week. I kept trying to think about how long it's been, then I tried to remember the last time I didn't feel crazy, or at least didn't *think about* feeling crazy, but I couldn't remember. I can't remember being with or without this feeling, and I started to wonder if I've always been this way. Then I stopped wondering, because I was starting to get to myself.

I wonder if my back looks any better. I haven't had a really good look at it, but the scarring looked raw and pale yesterday morning. Yesterday? I can't remember if it was yesterday. Maybe the day before. Or last week? *Oh God. What is that?* A bristly patch of hairs, almost identical to my paintbrush-like leg hair, has sprung up on my back, right where the scarring was. As if fertilised by it.

Running my fingers through and around the patch, I can feel smaller baby hairs all across my back, waiting for their moment to grow. I instinctively whip my head away from the mirror, wanting nothing more than to smash it into a thousand tiny pieces. I look down at my feet. And I've barely had time to recover from the back-hair shock when I notice my toenails – there seems to be a gnarled black shape under each one. I drop to the ground and hunch closer to my toes, then immediately feel sick. These black shapes push my toenails upward, so that they hover ever so slightly above my toes, as if waiting to either rot or snap clean off. Craning my neck to get a better look, I can see that each black shape is the same thing. Underneath my toenails are a set of curled, deformed claws.

Don't scratch your back. *Don't scratch your back.* You'll be better off if you ignore it, if you just learn to live with it. Don't let the itch control you. *You control the itch.*

Look around you. Everybody in this classroom wants you to scratch at that itch until there's blood oozing down your back, and they can point and whisper and snigger and feel safe knowing they're not the 'other' today.

Well, they're going to be waiting.

My room doesn't look right. Did Dad move something while I was out? What's different? It smells different. Someone's definitely been in here.

Argh, my neck.

I know people on the bus saw me twitching earlier.

What the hell did Dad do to my room? Is it my bedside table? Did he move my books around? What about my desk? Is all my homework still there? Where the fuck has he put my maths textbook? I tell him a thousand times not to go into my room or touch my stuff, and what does he do the second I leave the house?

They can put on an act, try to pretend I'm welcome, but I know there's this layer of resentment, barely below the surface. Nobody addresses it, nobody talks about it. They don't *have* to say it though, because I know they're thinking it. *It's so obvious.*

I wish they'd just leave one morning and never come back, and I could just stay here with the whole house to myself and I could go anywhere and do anything and there'd be no questions or judgement or obligations.

It'd just be me, happy and alone.

I don't need to be here. I don't know why I didn't see it months ago, but I genuinely don't. I don't enjoy it here. I don't understand anything anyone says to me. Nobody here me wants me to be here. I've thought this before, I've definitely thought it, but right now *I know.* And I know that *they know.*

Just stand up and walk out. Don't listen to anyone calling your name – they don't care – just keep walking out until you reach those doors.

I can feel that lovely tingling under my skin again.

Good, Tori. Don't look back.

I used to imagine this park near my old house was the bush. I'd run into the trees and crouch down, and I wouldn't be able to see any of the pathways or dogs being walked or my parents calling for me to come out. I'd hide in there for as long as I could get away with and just pretend I was lost in the outback and had to survive for as long as possible.

Sometimes Rebecca would pretend, too. We'd look for 'food' and we'd build bundles of sticks for 'fire' and we'd drop to the ground and hide from anybody who passed close by. Pretend they were dingoes or bushmen coming to get us. Sometimes I would stay there until after Rebecca had to go home to her parents, and I'd watch the sun go down and fall asleep against the trees, in some random spot near the back of the park.

Lying down in that same spot feels so much more claustrophobic now. Most of the trees and bushes in the park have been trimmed, but my spot has been neglected. It's gone feral. Branches scrape and scratch against my face as I lie here now. Looking out of the mess of overhanging branches arched around me, I can't remember how I ever felt comfortable enough to sleep here.

I just want to make it all go away. The stream-of-consciousness, the self-loathing, the uncertainty. The perpetual feeling like something horrible's always seconds away from happening to me. And that stupid fucking itch, burrowing around under my skin, making it impossible for me to do anything.

I look into the mirror and try to recognise something about myself: Dad's jacket, the scar from when I tried to give myself my first piercing, the birthmark on my ... *Shit, where is my birthmark?* God, that's stupid, why can't I remember where my ...? I swear it's always been right here, on my left arm. Or was it my right arm? I don't know.

I know my arms used to be longer. I know I used to have

longer arms. And I used to sleep well and go out for runs every second morning. I used to get my homework done at my best friend's house and spend the night because it was easier than walking home. My best friend. What's her name again? *Rachel. Ramona. Reagan.* Christ, why can't I remember? I remember having a patch of hair on my back. Was that real? Is it still there?

I swivel in the mirror to look. My entire torso – no, nearly my entire body – is covered by a thick coat of bristly, matted hair. No, it can't be hair. *It's feathers.* I can feel the quills as I run my fingers through my plumage. I feel dirt and dried mud and insects and hot water.

My toenails. My shoes and socks have to come off. Oh god, there's that itch again – and the tingle as I scratch it – both at once, fighting for control of me. My toenails are cracked: most of them have already come off, leaving my toes bloody and raw, with litterings of lint. *Jesus.* My toes are starting to fuse together, creating three large, distended claws, my skin peeling off to reveal a scaly, bloody pink underneath.

Stabbing pain in my neck and my whole body careens forward; I have to stop myself from crashing head-first into my mirror. I feel the vertebrae in my spine shuffling and rearranging as my neck convulses. Want to call out for Mum, but no noise escapes my mouth. Grab onto the sink for support. *Look up at yourself. It's going to be okay.*

Something in my back is ripping violently. I can't hear myself grunting, but I can feel it in my chest and rumbling the floor. The itch is killing me now. I just want to pull out those scissors and cut my spine out. *Perspective shifting, eyes going fuzzy, can barely stand up.*

Need to look at myself.

Need to look at myself in the mirror.

Grab the sink and look at yourself.

My jaw and cheeks bend and break into a beak-like shape, bones snapping and shattering. Meeting my own gaze in the mirror, I tremble and quiver. But even though this is the worst pain I have ever felt, my eyes look resigned to the pain in my body, and I know I'll be okay if I just embrace the pain and try not to think about it. My arms are shrivelling and withering into thin air. *Don't dwell on it. Don't let the pain control you.* Can see my pores opening up, feathers blooming. My knees threaten to give way as I feel my bone, skin, muscle: expanding and reducing all over. *Don't think about it, Tori. Just relax.* The itch finally fades, and the tingling returns.

I see it all in the mirror, everything moving into place: my neck extending, my spinal cord bending, my head shrinking, my feet becoming claws attached to two long, scaly legs. The pain comes back. *Stop thinking about it.* Large, beady eyes remain, staring through me in the mirror, watching as if from a distance. Just have to stare back, shut out everything else, and let my thoughts fade away.

What's happened to me? *It's going to be okay.* What colour is that? *Just accept it all.* Where did I come from to get here? *Just let it all fade away.* What was I so sad about?

Just let it all fade away.

Rappaccini's Son

HOLDEN SHEPPARD

It's in a place of beauty that I discover some feelings are uglier than others.

Being a high-school dropout in an isolated Midwest town doesn't offer brilliant prospects, but I've landed on my feet. I work as a storeman and delivery boy for Flowers by Pietro, a florist's in a local shopping centre, filled with the beauty of orchids, daffodils and roses. Pietro is an old Italian bloke who smokes a pack a day but still smells more like ouzo than tobacco due to the tiny bottle he carries in his grubby tracksuit pants. Even though the company is only Pietro, his wife Lisabetta, and me, it's the second-biggest florist in town.

Pietro comes to work one Monday more jolly than usual, a spring in his step as he whistles an Italian folk song.

'Lemme guess. AC Milan won last night's game?' I ask, dragging a bucket of roses out of the coolroom.

'Even better,' he says. 'Joe Rappaccini is dead.'

Rappaccini's is the biggest florist in town – Pietro's bitter rival and former business partner.

'Oh shit. That's horrible.'

Pietro gives me a beady-eyed glare that could wither all ten roses in my bucket. 'Don't be a *stronzo*, Giovanni. This is the best day of my life.'

I know my face betrays my horror, because he goads me further, kicking my bucket with his worn sneakers. 'You're soft, Giovanni. You don't understand the world.'

'I just don't feel good about someone else being dead. Shouldn't you feel compassion, even for your enemies, once they're dead?'

Pietro pours a shot of ouzo.

'Rappaccini was a bastard,' he says simply, like this is as empirical as the price of tulips. 'He betrayed me. If I carked it first, he'd be as happy as I am now.' He frowns at me. 'Don't pretend to be a saint, Giovanni. Nobody is. And the people who pretend are always the ones to watch out for.'

My first delivery run of the day includes a bouquet of white lilies, along with a card to the Rappaccini family. The sender's address is the same as ours.

'You're sending his family flowers?' I ask Pietro, bewildered.

'Of course.' He ashes his cigarette. 'He was my enemy, but I still honour him.' As I'm trying to process that, he adds, 'And when you deliver them, see if you can spot the body. Would be good to know that mongrel's really dead.'

I ride my scooter out from the shopping centre car park,

down the main street of town. The girl at the bank waves to me as always. The girl at the bakery calls out, 'Hey, Italian boy!' and I call back, 'Ciao, bella!' At the grocer's, a blond guy with a tattoo sleeve is setting out crates of carved-up watermelon and pumpkin. I only look at him when his back is turned. I wonder if he looks at me as I ride away.

I do my deliveries and leave the lilies until last. I feel a resistance to it, like delivering Pietro's insincere gift is giving someone poison when they asked for medicine.

I ride my scooter to a large rural property ten kilometres out of town, among orchards where Vietnamese market gardeners grow tomatoes and Italian families grow olives. The Rappaccini homestead is old red brick set on several hectares, but it's dwarfed by the garden behind it – easily the biggest garden I've ever seen. Out here, the sun belts down and the soil is crumbly and dry, but the Rappaccinis' garden is all *green* – unnaturally green for an Aussie summer. It's much lusher than the house itself, which has an abandoned feel to it. Grime covers the windows. Thick red dust coats the letterbox. Concentric golden orb spider webs hang between the palm trees and the decaying fascia of the porch. There's no sign of life. The Camry station wagon in the carport looks like it used to be white but it's now the colour of sour custard.

I ring the doorbell, but there's no sound. I knock on the door instead, coating my knuckles with red dust. I wipe them on my navy-blue work shorts.

After I knock the second time, I start to feel uneasy. The place is too quiet, like the whole house is holding its breath. I glance back at my scooter, comforted to see it still parked on the gravel – an escape if I need it.

'Hello?' I call. 'Delivery from Pietro's.'

Maybe there's nobody here. I don't know if Joe Rappaccini even had a family. Maybe I'm just meant to drop the lilies and bail.

I knock one more time. Nothing.

There's no sound here – that's the weird thing. Anywhere else, you'd have birds chirping, bees humming, dragonflies vibrating. But the moment I shut off my scooter, all I could hear was the wind.

Something touches my shoulder and I jump, thinking it's a golden orb spider. But it's just a frond from the bush beside the door; a slender protrusion, curly like a vine, with fat leaves.

I step away from the vine, and check the cobwebs just to be safe, but they're all empty. Even the spiders have fled this place.

I decide to follow the spiders' example and hightail it out of here. If this place is too creepy for them, it's definitely too creepy for me. I place the lilies at the base of the door and tuck the envelope from Pietro into the security screen.

The door creaks open, just an inch.

I step back. 'Hello?'

It's too dark to see beyond the door.

'I have a delivery from Pietro's,' I call, sounding more confident than I feel.

The vine brushes my shoulder again and I jump away. How can it keep reaching me when I keep backing further away from it?

Finally, I hear a voice within the house say, 'The door's open.'

For a bizarre moment it sounds like my own voice: the timbre of a teenager, mostly Aussie but a hint of Italian inflection.

'Flower delivery,' I call through the flywire. 'I'll leave it at the door.'

'No,' the other boy says, voice so like mine. 'They're flowers for my father, aren't they? Bring them to me. It would be rude to just leave them outside.'

I bristle, not out of fear but from the way he says *bring them to me*, like a command rather than a request. I don't owe him anything. I could drop these flowers and run, which is what the tingling at the back of my neck wants me to do.

But this is Joe Rappaccini's son. He just lost his father. I don't know how I'd function if I lost my father. The least I can do is deliver Pietro's fake-sympathy flowers in person.

So I push the door open and step into the gloom.

Nobody's swept the floor inside for a long time, maybe years. It's as dirty as most people's patios, strewn with red dust and fallen leaves that haven't curled up and died, but are still green, just disembodied. I wonder if this is just what a florist's house looks like. I don't think it is.

'I'm out the back,' the boy calls.

I follow his voice down a dark, windowless corridor. The gloom presses in on my sides. I feel like a nascent bug being drawn into the syrupy jaws of a Venus fly-trap.

The corridor opens up into a kitchen littered with dirty dishes, takeaway containers and crumpled cans. A pizza box is open, strewn with stale crusts, but there are no ants on it.

An open sliding door leads into a lush courtyard, and this is where I see the boy. He's on a wicker chair beneath a pergola covered in grapevines and creeping ivy. The courtyard looks like a nursery left to grow out of control. A kidney-shaped marble fountain is full of stagnant water, suffocated by algae and overgrown lily pads. The garden's trees and ferns are monstrous, their leaves forming a canopy so only dappled light reaches the terracotta pavers below. Flowers with petals broader than dinner plates disgorge from planter boxes.

I step over the threshold.

'Who are the flowers from?' the boy asks brusquely. 'Nobody liked my father.'

He has the deep Italian looks I inherited from my own father – eyes of polished black marble, swarthy olive skin – but his hair is curlier than mine, clinging to his head like Vantablack moss. And the tired circles around his eyes, like smears of charcoal, are much darker than his curls: he looks like he's been haunted as long as he's been alive.

'They're from his old business partner, Pietro,' I say, holding out the bouquet. 'I'm just the messenger,' I add. *As in, don't shoot me.*

'Oh, that Pietro.' The boy takes the bouquet, sneers at the lilies. 'Nobody hated my father more than him.' He raises the largest lily to his nose and takes a deep sniff. His eyes roll back, like the scent got him high. 'Yeah, I can smell that. These flowers reek with envy and contempt. Pietro sent these as a final *fuck you* to my father.'

As he clutches the bouquet, the lilies begin to wither. At first I think I'm imagining it, but within seconds, each flower loses its stark contrast of white on green, fading to sepia. The moisture leeches out of their stems and petals until they crumble completely and sprinkle like dust onto the terracotta.

Some of the dust lands on my dirty sneakers. I shake it off, like it's poison.

'How did you do that?' I say breathlessly.

The boy tosses the bouquet's empty cellophane to the floor. He seems unfazed, like making flowers die in his hands is as normal as picking them. Above his head, three yellow buds on a tree open up, blossoming like sunlight just touched them for the first time.

'I didn't do that,' the boy says. 'Pietro did. Sending pure hate at me. The bastard.'

He scares me. I want to run, but I fear making a sudden movement. I can't get over those flowers being desiccated into dust. And I can never stand up for myself at the best of times. I survive uncomfortable situations by swallowing my feelings and being as polite as possible.

'I'm sure Pietro didn't mean anything bad. The flowers were to pay his respects to your father.'

The boy laughs and it rings of triumph, like when you've been fishing for a long time and finally feel something tugging on the line. 'The way you defend your boss is very . . . wholesome,' he says slowly. He's looking at me intensely, eyes flicking across my body the way I looked at the blond bloke at the grocer's this morning. 'What's your name?'

'I'm just the delivery boy. I'm no relation to Piet—'

'I didn't ask who you were related to. I asked your name.'

I shiver. His voice is so like mine. Too young to be so authoritative and cold. Something about him makes me feel like my skin isn't mine.

'My name is Giovanni.'

'Good Italian name. I'm Santino, but everyone calls me Sonny, like the son in *The Godfather*.'

I know that movie. Every Italian kid does. My father loves it. So does Pietro. The character Sonny is a violent hothead. The tingle of my gut tells me this Sonny's no different.

'Good to meet you, but I've got more deliveries to make, or Pietro will be mad . . .'

I start to slowly back away. Sonny watches me without moving.

'Heaven forbid you make Pietro mad, hey, Giovanni?'

I freeze. 'He's my boss.'

'I bet you've never made anyone mad in your life, have you?'

'Why would I want to?'

Sonny's dark eyes are fixed on mine, almost hypnotically. There is something I like about his eyes. If I weren't so frightened by him, I would want to keep staring into them.

'No reason.' He claps his hands. 'Well, I'd better let you go, huh?'

He says it in a way that makes me feel he is physically releasing me from capture.

'Thanks. Later.'

I head back towards the sliding door into the house, but Sonny calls after me.

'Wait, Giovanni. Can you give old Pietro a message for me?'

My skin shivers, but I turn back. 'Yeah, of course. What is it?'

'Tell him to go fuck himself.'

'I can't say that.'

'Sure, you can. It's not you saying it. It's me. You're just the messenger, right?'

I manage a tiny, non-committal nod and escape through the house as fast as I can. When I reach the front porch, I pass the vine that tapped me on the shoulder earlier. It's grown so long, it's touching the ground.

I don't tell Pietro what Sonny said. Sonny's right: I don't wanna make anyone mad. I guess I was raised that way. I don't see why anyone would *deliberately* do the wrong thing. So the next day, when Pietro asks me how the visit went, I just confirm I dropped the flowers off.

'But what did Santino say when you said they were from *me*?' Pietro ashes his cigarette. His eyes are greedy, pregnant. Sonny was right. The flowers were a gloat.

I busy myself with hosing a bucket clean. 'I don't think he knew how to take it.'

'Bull!' Pietro says. 'He knew exactly how to take it. That boy's as much of a bastard as his father. Weird kid.'

I can't fault him there. I lay awake last night thinking about Sonny, wondering how those flowers shrivelled up and died in his hands. But what unnerved me more was Sonny himself. The way he talked about people like he didn't give a shit about them, even his dead father. The way his garden flourished after he destroyed that bouquet.

And I can't stop thinking about what he said: that I've never made anyone mad. Until yesterday, I was proud of that. But Sonny made it sound like a weakness.

I dwell on it all day. I start to notice stuff that, usually, I would just consider part of the natural order.

The way Pietro barks orders at me, kicks things in my direction, calls me names in either English or Italian depending on how angry he is with me.

The way his wife, Lisabetta, rolls her eyes at me, calls me slow and clumsy and refers to me as Shrek when she introduces me to her friend from the jeweller's shop.

I am a joke to these people. I cop flak daily and I never tell anyone off for it. I hunch my shoulders when objects or insults are hurled at me. I laugh when I am insulted, as if the joke at my expense was indeed funny. I absorb the world's hate like a sponge that is never wrung out. And somehow, I've never noticed.

On my last delivery run of the day, I wonder what would happen if I didn't wave to the banker. If I didn't say 'Ciao, bella!' to the bakery girl. If I told the bloke at the grocer's what I really think about his muscled arms.

Those thoughts shouldn't make me feel good, but they send an electric thrill down my spine and into my tailbone.

When I ride back to Pietro's, the old man is smoking at the back of the shop. 'Late delivery came through.' He jabs his half-ashed cigarette at a bouquet of red roses in a white bucket.

'But I knock off at five.' The words come out in a tone I've never used.

Pietro raises an eyebrow. 'You givin' me attitude, son? I pay you for one job. You deliver the bloody flowers.'

'I'm meant to be going home now,' I mutter, kicking the side of the flower bucket.

'Like you got anything to do at home except jerk off.' Pietro flicks his smoke to the ground, stomps on the butt. 'Do as you're told.'

I don't want to lose my job, so I grab the bouquet. 'You're kidding me?' I reread the address. 'The Rappaccini house again?'

'Quit talking back.'

A knot tightens in my gut as I examine the roses. 'People usually send lilies for a death, don't they?'

Pietro's pouring himself an ouzo and Coke. 'You don't tell people what flowers to send. You just deliver them.'

I ride to the Rappaccini estate, the knot of dread pulling

tighter in my stomach the closer I get. What looked green by day looks black by night. There are no lights on inside: dark windows gape like the open eyes of a corpse.

I cut the scooter's engine. I consider dropping the bouquet at the door and sprinting away without knocking. The boy in that garden terrifies me.

At the same time, I feel unable to move my feet. Something stronger than fear gnaws at my chest: a curious hunger. Sonny saw my soul like nobody else has. I want to know what else he can see. Maybe I want to see something in him, too.

So, I knock.

He answers within a second. 'Jeez, you took your time, Giovanni.' Sonny's voice carries down the corridor from the courtyard garden. Was he able to see me standing on the porch this whole time?

'You have another delivery,' I call. 'I'll leave them here for you. Have a good night.'

'Come on, Giovanni. You can't just leave them outside. Bring them to me.'

I already knew he'd order this. I wanted him to, because then it wasn't me choosing to go inside that garden. He was forcing me.

The door creaks open. This time, I see the vine protruding from the bush; it's snaked around the bottom of the door and pulled it open for me, like it has a mind of its own. I imagine this isn't really happening. I stare at the vine, scared to step over it in case it snares my foot.

'It won't hurt you, Giovanni,' Sonny calls. 'Come in.'

I want to go inside just a fraction more than I want to run away.

The house is as dirty as yesterday, except by night, the edges of the decay aren't visible. It makes me imagine monsters looming in the shadows.

Sonny is on his chair in the courtyard, olive skin blueish in the moonlight. He's scrolling on his phone as I step into the garden. I clear my throat and he still doesn't look up, remaining focused on his phone.

He's deliberately ignoring me even after inviting me in. What a prick.

As annoying as that is, I'm envious. I wish I could be as rude and callous as him.

'I brought your flowers,' I announce. 'Later.'

Sonny looks up with a smirk. 'Roses? For me? Giovanni, you shouldn't have.'

Sparks race down my spine. 'They aren't from me.'

Sonny jerks his head at the bouquet. 'Are you sure? What does the card say?'

My face flushes with a guilt I don't own. He's making me think I sent these roses to him, but I know I didn't. Why would I?

The envelope is addressed *Bello*. The paper is dry against my clammy hands.

'Open it,' Sonny commands.

The front of the card shows a puppy holding out a bulging red love-heart. The inside reads:

Giovanni,
A dozen red roses for the most beautiful boy I've ever laid eyes on.
Sono pazzo di te, bello.
Santino

My heart races, like I've been caught breaking out of prison. I'm waiting for floodlights, barking guard dogs, a gunshot in the back.

I look up. Sonny's black eyes are locked with mine. I can't take my eyes off him.

'You're mad about me?' I translate, numb. 'You don't even know me.'

'I know enough,' Sonny says, swallowing so his Adam's apple bounces almost as violently as my heart in my rib cage. 'I know you're like me. I can tell.'

'How could you possibly know that?'

'The flowers speak for themselves,' Sonny says.

Since I read his card, something has happened to the bouquet in my hand. The roses have blossomed more, petals open wide, growing more richly red, as if blood is rushing through their stems.

'How are you doing that?' I say. 'The garden. How are you making this happen? Is it a trick?'

'My father's garden feeds off the darkness inside the heart,' Sonny says, still calmly seated.

'That's crazy. Are you in a cult or something?'

'No cult. Not crazy. Just the truth. Some people pretend they're flawless. My father never did. He embraced his flaws the way most people fear to. His garden responded to that.'

'You don't seem to miss him much. Why aren't you more upset?'

'I guess he taught me how to live in my darkness, too. My father wasn't a nice man. I'm not a nice boy. He wouldn't cry for me if I died. I won't cry for him.'

His emotionless tone frightens me, but I'm drawn to him. There's a strength in his frozen heart that I want to understand.

'Your boss gets it,' Sonny goes on. 'Pietro wasn't afraid to send that bouquet to me. Schadenfreude at someone else's death is a dark emotion, but he didn't pretend not to feel it. You pretend, though, Giovanni. You pretend to be a good boy. You never passed on my message.'

'I couldn't. Pietro's not perfect, but he's a good man.'

'Bollocks. You're worse than Pietro. Worse than my father. You deny the darkness in you.' He breathes in through his nostrils, like he's trying to inhale me. 'That's what makes you so intoxicating.'

'Intoxicating?'

'Your boy-scout act fools everyone else, but not me. I can see your darkness. It only gets stronger the more you try to deny it. And you deny more than most. When you came here yesterday, I felt energised. Your darkness is deeper than anyone's. You're like a present under a Christmas tree. I've never wanted to unwrap something more in my life.'

I swallow. I don't know how he can see right into me like this.

'I don't know what darkness you're on about, mate. I've only been having these thoughts since I met you.'

'No,' Sonny says. 'I only unlocked what was already in you. Normal emotions you're hell-bent on denying. Vengeance. Rage. Lust. My garden senses it in you. It responds, see?'

He gestures at my feet, where weeds are sprouting up in real time through the cracks in the terracotta. Their stems are ripe as they stretch higher than my ankle. I am living fertiliser for this dark place.

'Make it stop,' I tell him.

'Why stop something so beautiful?' Sonny says, mouth curling. 'You should hang out with me more often, *bello*. Any feeling is allowed here. You don't have to pretend to be good. You can be yourself.'

'I am not darkness,' I say, even though this is what I am most afraid of. That I am what Sonny says I am: vengeful, lustful, angry. That if I unleashed any of those feelings, I would never be able to stop them.

'We are all darkness, Giovanni. Your darkness would be safe with mine.'

I feel an itching under my skin. I'm scared that if I stay a second longer, I'd be willing to flay myself alive just to scratch it. 'I have to go.'

Sonny raises an eyebrow. 'Okay. But you'll be back.'

'No, I won't.'

'Have you ever received flowers from another boy before?'

'Never.'

'Nor have I. How did it feel?' He watches my face as I fall silent. 'Tell me. I'll know whether you're lying or not.'

I clutch the roses. They've doubled in size since I delivered them. 'I didn't like it. And I don't want them.'

I drop the bouquet among the weeds. The stems immediately sprout roots, engorging and digging into the gaps beneath the pavers. The rosebuds glow so bright-red they are almost luminescent.

Sonny smiles. 'You lied.' He folds his arms. 'But it felt good to be cruel to my face, didn't it? You didn't even try to spare my feelings. You're as dark as I thought.'

'I'm leaving.'

'Do whatever you think will hurt me most. Be a bastard. What a rush, hey?'

'I'm not trying to hurt you.' I gesture to the garden, looking at the weird boy in the chair. 'I don't know what this place is, but I don't want to come back. Bye.'

I head back into the house. I need to get out of here. I'm losing my mind.

'You still have to do one thing, Giovanni,' Sonny calls. 'Tell Pietro to go fuck himself.'

'I'm not your messenger boy.'

'It's not a message from me,' Sonny taunts. 'It's a message from you.'

I can't get Sonny out of my head.

Not just his beautiful eyes and his handsome face, which surface, unbidden, in my dreams.

What I can't shake is what he said to me. What he said is inside me. I know I'm not darkness. I'm good. I want to be good, even if my core is secretly like rotten grapefruit.

The following day, I try to forget what happened and move on. But when I rock up to Pietro's, the old man is in a foul mood and ready to take it out on me.

'Here's the *stronzo* now,' he mutters to Lisabetta as he mixes brandy into his coffee. He clips me around the ears as I pass. 'What did you forget yesterday, dickhead?'

I'm used to being clipped over the ears – whether it's Pietro or my father – but this time it feels unfair. Pietro gestures to the buckets of flowers that were left out in the shop overnight, rather than being put away in the coolroom.

'You told me to do that late delivery to the Rappaccini house.'

'You still shoulda put away the stock.' Pietro sips the brandy-coffee. 'Look how wilted they are! And you forgot to sweep up.'

He hands me a broom. I take it, burning with unspoken rage.

I start to sweep but Pietro clicks his tongue. 'Put some oomph into it, *stronzo*.'

Lisabetta prepares the cash register, rolling her eyes. 'Slow as a tortoise, that boy.'

I sweep the store while muttering curse words in my head. But they aren't my most toxic thoughts. I keep seeing images of me finally exploding. Shouting at Lisabetta that she's more useless than me since she can't even log in to the computer without my help. Clipping Pietro over the ears, telling him he's a prick and an alcoholic and that I wish he was dead.

The thoughts keep spiralling all day. Every time Pietro or Lisabetta give me a task, there is always a sneer, either on their face or buried in their tone. I start thinking about how I would kill them if I had the power. I imagine luring them into Sonny's garden, where the plants come alive in my presence. How Pietro's sneer would die on his face when my vines choked him and lifted him off the ground, smashing his frail skull into the terracotta. How Lisabetta would scream as I fed her to a giant Venus fly-trap that swallowed her whole.

Once or twice, I shake my head. I would never hurt anyone. Never. I'm placid. Kind. Giovanni, the gentle giant. Shrek.

These aren't my thoughts.

Or are they?

Just before my first delivery run, the doorbell jingles and a woman enters the shop. It's the girl from the bank. She's come in to get a bouquet for her workmate's birthday.

As she's paying Lisabetta, she spots me. 'Oh! I hoped I'd see you here. You know, us girls at the bank all think you're cute as a button.'

Cute as a button. Like a puppy. All adults look at me like a dumb little kid.

'Thanks,' I mutter.

'What's your name, buddy?'

'Giovanni.'

'That's a cute name.' She smiles. 'I'm Laura.'

'Giovanni isn't cute,' Lisabetta says, handing back her change. 'It's Italian for "John". It's boring and plain. Anyway, he answers to Shrek, because he's as clumsy as an ogre. Isn't that right, Shrek?'

Laura laughs before leaving with a wave. I feel a surge of fury at Lisabetta.

'At least I don't *look* like an ogre,' I blurt out. 'Wish I could say the same for you.'

Lisabetta's jaw drops. 'What did you just say to me?'

'Only what you said to me.' It feels good to not absorb her scorn. Revenge served in the heat of the moment; an eye for an eye. This is power.

'I'm telling Pietro about this.'

'Knock yourself out.'

I head out on my delivery run. Laura waves; I speed past her without waving back. The bakery girl calls, 'Hey, Italian boy!' and I reply, 'Ciao, *brutta*!' I grin savagely as I speed past, wondering if she knows the Italian word for ugly.

At the grocer's, I pull up to perve on the blond guy with the tattoos. His biceps flex as he unloads a crate of peaches. He glances up, notices me staring. 'Can I help you?'

'Just checking out your guns, bro. Impressive.'

'Um . . .' He looks totally confused. 'Thanks, I s'pose? Sorry, do I know you from the gym or something?'

'Not yet. You wanna go out some time? Get to know me better?'

His face sours. 'What the hell? I'm not into that.' Sour turns to bitter. 'Get out of here.'

I shrug. 'Whatever you say, man.'

I watch as the peaches start to engorge, swelling to twice their normal size, then explode, one by one. Sweet, tiny bombs, splattering their flesh all over the blond guy. He shouts in alarm and stares up at me.

I restart the scooter's motor with a wild grin. A fly buzzes around my face, a constant needling. I breathe at it. The fly freezes in mid-air and drops to the ground, dead. Good. I am what Sonny said I am. He's made me strong.

When I return to the florist's, Pietro greets me with folded arms and a scowl.

'How dare you insult my wife!' he roars. 'That's not the Giovanni I know. You cut it out. Now.'

I square my jaw at him, jutting it out like I'm begging him to hit me. 'This *is* the real me, Pietro.'

Pietro loads a bouquet into my scooter's basket for my next run. 'Well, *the real you* better apologise to my wife, if *the real you* wants to keep his job.'

I look at this withered, addicted old man who has kept me down for so long, and my lip curls of its own accord. 'Hey, Pietro. Go fuck yourself.'

Pietro reaches out to clip me around the ears. I block him and grip the bones in his wrists like I'm trying to pull his arms off. I want to shout. I want to thrash, throw him around the shop, bounce him off the walls like a rag doll. I want vines to string him up, draw and quarter him until his limbs rip from their sockets in a crimson rain of blood. I want to destroy him.

The gurgling draws me back to reality. Pietro has collapsed to his knees while my hands maintain their vice grip around his wrists. His skin is thin and papery, white as a death lily. His veins are engorged, pumping with deoxygenated blood, blue spiderwebs surfacing on every part of his body. His eyes are stained red and his lips dry out and crack open.

My touch is draining the life out of him. He's dying.

Only when his bloodshot eyes flutter shut and he falls limp does the electricity shoot through my spine. A part of me I'd forgotten surges back, desperate not to die with Pietro.

I release him. His body drops to the polished concrete.

'Pietro!' I shout.

The old man coughs. His bloodshot eyes blink open and he stares at me in terror.

'I'm sorry,' I say. 'I'm so sorry. I never meant to hurt you. I never wanted to hurt anyone.'

Pietro clutches his throat and calls for Lisabetta.

Instinctively, I grab the keys to my scooter and flee. I know where I need to go.

The sun is scorching when I reach the Rappaccini house. I dismount my scooter and grab the bouquet, striding for the door. I don't knock: the vine responds to my arrival, curling around the front door and throwing it open.

I surge through the corridor, through the kitchen and into the courtyard.

The wicker chair is empty. A rose bush, borne from the bouquet I dropped last night, has spread over the entire garden. The roses choke out the creepers, dangle into the fountain, even dig their thorns into the bark of the trees, like parasites feasting on flesh.

'Sonny! Where are you?'

His voice calls back like an echo. 'Where I'm supposed to be.'

I run through the garden, unsure if the voice is a beacon or a siren. Roses blossom alongside me as I run, almost chasing me.

Sonny is at the rear of the garden, kneeling beside a headstone laid atop a mound of fresh earth. His hands are clasped in prayer, eyelids closed. From within the grave, an enormous, pulsing green stalk has erupted. It snakes out of the soil, back into the garden, feeding it.

The name on the headstone is Joe Rappaccini.

'Your father is buried here?'

The roses have followed me, twisting themselves into an overhead canopy, throwing Sonny and me into shadow.

'He wanted to be buried at the cemetery, beside my mother,' Sonny says, not opening his eyes. 'I lied and told my family he wished to be buried here.'

'That's a cruel thing to do to a dead man.'

'The dead man *was* a cruel man. I am his cruelty.'

I feel sick. 'Sonny, what have you done to me?'

'Nothing. You did it to yourself. I just helped you embrace who you really are. And look at my garden now. You make it grow.'

'My darkness isn't who I am. And it's not who you are, either. Your father put that darkness in you.'

Sonny opens his dark, honey-trap eyes and smiles sadly. 'You know this because your father did the same to you. You can either be destroyed by his rejection, or grow stronger from it.'

'How do you know about my father?'

'I saw my pain in yours the moment I met you. We are alike because we love men. But we are also alike because of the men who should have loved us and didn't. Your father abandoned you once he saw what kind of boy you were, didn't he?'

I swallow the burning lump in my throat. 'My father works away. He doesn't have much time for . . .'

I can't finish the sentence.

'You know it in your gut, Giovanni,' Sonny says. 'All boys know, in our guts, whether or not our fathers approve of us as men. And if they don't, that wound is worse than death.'

The base of my neck tingles. The green stalk protruding from Rappaccini's grave pulses sickeningly. 'Pietro never told me, Sonny . . . how did your dad die?'

A tear slides down Sonny's cheek. 'He found out. Saw me looking at one of his workers. He could tell what I was. He was disgusted. And he disowned me.'

The image of Pietro choking for air flashes into my mind as I realise how Joe Rappaccini's life ended. 'Sonny, you didn't . . .'

'My father taught me to get revenge,' Sonny says, not bothering to wipe his face. 'You don't turn the other cheek. If someone hurts you, you hurt them back. So, I got him back.'

The green stalk pulses ominously. Joe Rappaccini's body is not resting. It is fertiliser for toxic rage.

I kneel down beside Sonny, look into his eyes. 'This garden isn't good for you. You need to get out of here.'

Sonny laugh-cries. 'Why would I leave? I've never felt stronger.'

'Stronger,' I repeat. 'But not happier.'

'Stronger is the way to survive.'

'Maybe I can help,' I say. 'We all have darkness, but we also have light. We can choose. Let me help you.'

'That's cute, Giovanni, but I'm too far gone.'

'We need to get you out of here. Come with me.'

Sonny shakes his head. 'Giovanni, the best thing you can do

is turn around and leave. Save yourself before I make you sick like me.'

'Your father doesn't get the last word on your character,' I say firmly. 'Listen to me, Sonny. I think you're good. I even brought you flowers.'

I hold up the bouquet that was meant to be one of my deliveries. Yellow roses, sunny and warm.

'I got you red roses, for love,' Sonny says, confused. 'You give me these instead. Yellow roses symbolise friendship.'

'Friendship is better than romance. More permanent.' I press the yellow blooms to his hands. 'For you, Sonny. From me. One good man to another.'

Sonny unclasps his hands. 'Giovanni. Don't. You don't know what you're doing.'

'If cruelty is the poison that made this garden,' I say, 'then mercy must be the antidote. Take them.'

I take his hands in mine, feel the warmth of our skin touching as I place the bouquet in his grasp. I tighten his hands over the stems and look deep into his eyes.

Tears stain his face. 'Giovanni. You idiot.' His whitened knuckles stroke the hair on my forearm. 'I could have loved you.'

My breath chokes on the past tense. 'Could have?'

The colour drains from his face. 'You were right. Mercy is the antidote to the poison.'

The hairs on the back of my neck stand up. 'That's a good thing, isn't it?'

Sonny's salt tears morph into blood.

'The garden isn't the poison, Giovanni. I am.'

Even as I clutch at him, I know it's too late. The yellow roses tumble. His eyes roll back in his head. I try to prop him up, but his body collapses to the dirt. The green stalk severs itself from the earth, rising out of the grave along with its toxic roots.

As I hold Sonny, the poison garden tears itself apart. Without its stalk, every plant withers, thrashes, screeches. The yellow roses glow with a light that pulses across the entire courtyard, until every fatal bloom bursts and dust rains to the floor.

The garden is no more. Only the red roses remain alive.

'Sonny.' I shake him. He has to be okay. Please, please let him be okay . . .

He shifts in my arms, but my relief is short-lived. Blood trickles from the corner of his mouth, from his abdomen. I wipe tears of blood from his face. He looks up at me, helpless, a seedling that won't survive. The antidote that annihilated the poison also annihilated him.

'I'm so sorry, Sonny. I was trying to save you.'

'But you did, Giovanni.' Sonny whispers. 'And I saved you. So, we're even.'

I lean close and feel his breath on mine. I touch the side of his face gently, until my fingertips sink into his curls and our lips meet. I kiss him. He kisses me back until he falls still. The rose canopy above drops its colour: red petals fall over us like sacred rain.

I wish I could have kissed him earlier. For longer: maybe forever. He tasted nothing like poison.

END NOTES

The Party
Wai Chim

Wai Chim is the Chinese-American-Australian author of a number of children's and YA titles, including the award-winning *The Surprising Power of a Good Dumpling*. Born and raised in New York, Wai now lives in Sydney with her husband and beloved cat, Freddie. She recently appeared as a contestant on *Australian Survivor*.

INSPIRATION

My inspiration for writing this story boils down to: '*2020 was the absolute pits. How could I make it worse?*' During such a difficult time, music and a strong online community helped carry me through what was really a creative blackhole. *The Party* is written as a homage and gentle nod to ARMY – I hope fans and non-fans alike will appreciate the final reveal.

Seek and Destroy
Jared Thomas

Dr Jared Thomas is a Nukunu person of the Southern Flinders Ranges and the Curator of Aboriginal and Torres Strait Islander Art and Material Culture at the South Australian Museum, and an international award-winning author.

INSPIRATION

'Seek and Destroy' was inspired by my love of the song 'Seek and Destroy' by the band Metallica and the story is basically a conglomeration of the type of stories my friends and I continue to tell each other when we're sitting around the fire. The idea for the story began with thinking about the tent scene. A friend and I shared a tent with a non-Aboriginal kid on school camp in Grade Five and we told him stories like the one about Georgie Barnes, featured in 'Seek and Destroy'. Consequently I slept with one eye open that night.

The country holds spirits and we need to be careful not to disturb them.

It's Quiet Now
Emma Preston

Emma Preston is an aspiring illustrator. She has completed her Bachelor of Design (Illustration Animation) and is currently working on illustrating children's books. Emma lives on the Fleurieu Peninsula and uses the landscape around her to inspire her works, including her graphic novel 'It's Quiet Now'.

INSPIRATION
The beginning of the year 2020's quarantine was a weird time for everyone. During this time, I was at university and still had classes to attend before the full lockdown. I remember walking around the city. It was quiet, and no one was around. But I still felt like I was being watched. It reminded me of when me and my family went camping out in the Flinders Ranges, which became the inspiration for this story.

As the lockdown begins, the cities grow silent.

Monsters who fear noise take solitude within the unpopulated areas of the Australian outback. But when people start to lock down, and cities and residential areas become quiet, these curious monsters decide to do some investigating. When the lockdown ends, however, streets become bustling once more and the monsters take refuge in alleyways.

Most leave, deciding that the noise is too much to bear. But some stay, having adapted to their new existence.

Heart-shaped Stone
Vikki Wakefield

Vikki Wakefield lives and writes in Adelaide. Her works include award-winning novels *All I Ever Wanted*, *Friday Brown*, *Inbetween Days* and *Ballad for a Mad Girl*, and her latest novel *This Is How We Change the Ending* was awarded the 2020 CBCA Book of the Year, Older Readers.

INSPIRATION

My love for horror began in my early teens, reading Jackson, Poe, Lovecraft, King and Barker, turning the pages by torchlight. I carry vivid images of creepy settings – the Moors, the dank streets of London, abandoned estates and sinister small towns – but none were as terrifying as my own suburban backyard. As kids we would explore a series of deep interconnected gullies, crawling through filthy stormwater pipes and drains, but we avoided one place: a large granite slab, stained with blood and scattered with bones, leading to a crevice in the hillside. According to legend, offer a sacrifice and you were granted a wish, but ask too much and you might wake missing a tooth or a toe. I still live in the area. The crevice has grown wider; the slab is still blackened with blood and littered with bones. Feral foxes? Kids like us, carrying on a decades-old urban legend? Or an ancient entity, trapped by creeping suburbia?

Heart-shaped Stone was sparked by the memory of this unsettling place. When Arlo trades parts of herself in exchange for belonging and vengeance, it speaks to my affinity with monsters – often more so than humans. In truly affecting horror I think we are both.

Stop Revive Survive

Sarah Epstein

Sarah Epstein has been a horror fan since her teens when she regularly terrorised friends with scary stories and Ouija boards at sleepovers. She once stayed overnight in a disused quarantine station in the hopes of being haunted. You'll find her binge-watching shows about zombies or aliens at her home in bayside Melbourne.

INSPIRATION

In 2018, I did a solo road trip up the Hume Highway to be with my dying dad in Sydney. It was a long and lonely drive, and my thoughts inevitably slid into dark places. I was worried about not making it in time. I was worried about fatigue. I was worried about pulling over, alone, to take breaks at isolated rest areas. Who or what might be lurking out there in wild bushland and dense pine forests, along those desolate back roads and scrubby plains? In my distressed emotional state, the beautiful Australian landscape took on a sinister edge and left me feeling vulnerable. This is what inspired my short story about two boys on a mercy dash, and a rest stop that goes awry.

Don't Look!

Lisa Fuller

Lisa Fuller is an award-winning Murri writer living in Canberra since 2006. She is trying to complete her PhD, lives in a renovators delight and is owned by a spoilt staffy. She spends her days trying to balance work and writing, battling her inner critic every step of the way.

INSPIRATION

'Don't Look!' is loosely based on a real event in my life. It was one of the most terrifying nights of my life, and I never stepped foot inside that house again. My cousin later admitted that she asked me to sleep over because she was scared to sleep there alone. She didn't warn me about its origins or anything else, because she knew I'd refuse to come. She was 100% right.

I think most of us have experienced that scary feeling of not being alone and wanting to look but fighting the urge. Yet, it's more terrifying when you can't see what's out there. I love and hate it when the monster stays in the shadows, never fully seen.

The story includes my community's beliefs that you should *never* look in those situations, and that our loved ones are never truly gone. Though we grieve their loss, we know they are always with us, especially when we need them most. All you have to do is trust your gut, and listen.

Nature Boy

Poppy Nwosu

Poppy Nwosu is the author of three YA rom-com novels, *Making Friends with Alice Dyson* (2019), *Taking Down Evelyn Tait* (2020), and *Road Tripping with Pearl Nash* (2021), and is the creator of *Hometown Haunts: #LoveOzYA Horror Tales* (a project supported by an Australia Council for the Arts grant).

INSPIRATION

I wrote 'Nature Boy' as a reaction to the overwhelming events of 2020, in the middle of which, I also had three people connected to me pass away. I often use fiction as a release for my emotions, and a way to process an experience without talking directly about it. Hence, the idea for the unravellings in my story.

While writing, I really didn't know what would happen when my protagonist witnessed an unravelling at the end. For a while I thought it would be a brutal thing of blood and guts, but then decided it would be like the stuffing coming out of a toy. It was only while listening to a favourite song by Nat King Cole (called 'Nature Boy') that I realised I wanted to end my story with hope.

I imagine the lyrics my main character sings at the end are from that song; *The greatest thing you'll ever learn is just to love and be loved in return.* To me, this represents those small moments of fierce beauty that still exist despite the sad times, and which make life worth living.

Slaughterhouse Boys

Emma Osborne

Emma Osborne is a queer fiction writer and poet from Melbourne, Australia. Their writing has appeared in *Uncanny Magazine*, *Nightmare Magazine*, *Apex Magazine*, *Queers Destroy Science Fiction*, *Pseudopod*, *Wastelands 3: The New Apocalypse*, the *Year's Best Australian Fantasy and Horror* and *GlitterShip*.

Emma lives in Melbourne with their two cats, Maze and Pancake. You can find them on Twitter as @redscribe.

INSPIRATION

'Slaughterhouse Boys' deeply represents the Australian country where I grew up – the party, with all of the drunkenness and chaos and horror, is something I attended on scores of occasions as a young kid. I wanted to explore the feeling of not-belonging that I felt as a queer kid, the feeling of wanting to be somewhere I could be myself, and the fear that being myself would bring rejection.

'Slaughterhouse Boys' also grapples with my discomfort with being an omnivore who nevertheless is deeply disturbed by factory farming and animal abuse. Meat and blood and toxic masculinity and queerness and acceptance all folded neatly into this story as I was writing it. In the story, meat is a precious rarity, and I wanted to look at the repercussions of that in terms of family, of permitted violence, and the weight of expectation.

I also really wanted to explore the choice of my character, Tom, to seek the approval of his blood family rather than removing himself from his life as he knows it, from what is uncomfortable but relative safety, at least for now. I'd like to think he makes it out eventually.

Euryhaline

Margot McGovern

Margot McGovern is an Adelaide-based author and horror film junkie. She holds a creative writing PhD from Flinders University and her debut novel *Neverland* (Penguin Random House Aus.) was shortlisted for the 2020 Adelaide Festival Awards for Literature and the 2015 Text Prize. You can find her on Instagram: @project_lectito.

INSPIRATION

In 'Euryhaline' a swimming champion becomes convinced there's something sinister out to get her in the pool at her elite new school. It's a story about adapting to a hostile, high-performance environment and the intense pressure we place on ourselves to succeed, particularly when we feel we don't fit in.

To me, Imposter Syndrome – with which I'm all too familiar – has always felt particularly maleficent for the way it seeks out the things that bring us the most joy and twists them into a source of anxiety and fear. I wanted to explore that in 'Euryhaline' by drawing on my terror of submerged machinery (submechanophobia) and things brushing against my legs in the water to manifest Tam's anxiety and self-doubt as something monstrous.

Hunger

Marianna Shek

Marianna Shek writes YA speculative fiction. She has a PhD in transmedia storytelling. In 2020, she was the winner of the CYA fiction prize and shortlisted for the Affirm Press Mentorship Award at Varuna House. Her stories have been published by *Space and Time Magazine*, Serenity Press and Griffith University.

INSPIRATION

As a child, I had an insatiable appetite. Growing up in Hong Kong, I was exposed to a weird and wonderful array of culinary delicacies. Fermented tofu, frog legs and chicken giblets were my favourite things to eat! Nowadays, we have a thriving foodie culture. People share their experiences of how certain flavours and scents bring back the memories of home. This is not my relationship with food. When I think about certain dishes, I'm hit by the sense of umami, and then I remember my greed, my craving to eat more and never being sated.

The premise for 'Hunger' is based on my childhood experience. In my family home, we had a shrine with statues of Buddha and a framed photo of my grandparents and great-grandparents. At the centre of the altar was a Swarovski crystal bowl. It was implicitly understood that the fresh fruit from the weekly groceries goes into the fruit bowl as an offering before consumption. One day, I couldn't wait and I stole a mango from my ancestors.

The story of 'Hunger' is my imaginings of the retribution based on the ghost stories I grew up with.

Do We See It All Now?
Michelle O'Connell

Michelle O'Connell is an artist from Adelaide, South Australia and a recent graduate of a Bachelor of Design (Illustration and Animation). She finds great comfort and happiness when she shares her creations and ideas with others. This is especially true if people can relate to her creations and know that they're not alone in the things they feel and experience. Expressing herself through art is her lifeline and passion.

INSPIRATION

My story is inspired by growing up being neurodivergent and undiagnosed. A girl experiences life through her own lens. Her understanding of the world and how she is treated is filtered through it, perceiving negative and dangerous situations as neutral and harmless until later.

While growing up, she sees glimpses of reality. Every life event cracks the lens she sees the word through, until she eventually sees it for how it really is.

Angel Eyes
Alison Evans

Alison Evans is the award-winning author of the YA novels *Euphoria Kids*, *Highway Bodies* and *Ida*, and is a contributor in the anthology *Kindred: 12 Queer #LoveOzYA Stories*. They live on the unceded lands of the Wurundjeri People.

INSPIRATION

When Poppy asked me to write something for this anthology, I started by thinking about the things that scare me the most. This has been a good strategy for my writing, and my first two books focused on two of my biggest fears. Body horror is a particularly frightening branch of horror to me.

The next step was figuring out what kind of question I wanted to explore.

The way puberty is talked about by adults is often in quite monstrous terms, but it's not a monstrous thing at all. It's a stage of life. What parallels could I draw in a story that had characters going through both voluntary and involuntary physical changes? With that in mind: what makes a monster?

Best Years of Your Life
Felix Wilkins

Felix Wilkins is a screenwriter and filmmaker based in Melbourne. When he's not sweating over how to portray himself in his own bio, he's likely to be watching horror movies or producing content for his production company, Yabba Films.

INSPIRATION

Whoever first used the phrase 'the best years of your life' in reference to adolescence is an unrelenting sadist, and possibly more qualified to be a horror writer than I or anyone else published in this anthology.

The constant state of hormone-fuelled physical and mental dysphoria, the feelings that seem to hit either in complete extremes or not at all, having to maintain relationships with family and friends in the midst of all this, and feeling absolutely powerless to change any of it. This is a time of transformation, a slow, lingering, painful transformation that is made a million times worse by the looming presence of the future constantly hanging above, obscuring the better version of yourself that you aspire to be and replacing it with a temperamental, depressive, unstable monster that you barely recognise.

So if this time is genuinely the 'best years of your life', then don't tell Tori, unless you want to ruffle a few feathers.

Rappaccini's Son
Holden Sheppard

Holden Sheppard's novel *Invisible Boys* (Fremantle Press, 2019) won accolades including the WA Premier's Prize for an Emerging Writer. His work has appeared in *Griffith Review, Westerly, 10 Daily* and *HuffPost*. In his downtime, Holden is a gym junkie and plays footy (AFL). He lives in Perth with his husband.

INSPIRATION
When I started brainstorming this story, I knew I wanted to tap into my own inner fears. What most horrified me growing up was the prospect of doing the wrong thing. Despite trying to be a good Catholic boy, my biggest fear as a teenager was that my core was rotten; that I was a bad boy: deviant, rude, weird, unlikable, not good enough.

During that brainstorming in late 2020, I was working out at the gym, earphones in, when I stumbled across a Fleetwood Mac song, 'Running Through the Garden'. I was captivated: the lyrics suggested a much bigger story. I listened to it on repeat and when I got home, I discovered Stevie Nicks apparently wrote it after being inspired by American novelist Nathaniel Hawthorne's 1844 short story 'Rappaccini's Daughter'.

After I read 'Rappaccini's Daughter', I was inspired, too. I wanted to tell a warped love story between two young men, adapting the poison garden of Hawthorne's tale, and Nicks' lyric, into a metaphor for my own fears: that tug-of-war between flowery virtue and the angry weed-like desire to behave badly. And so, 'Rappaccini's Son' was born, a way to make Giovanni face his demons around his self-actualisation.

Road Tripping with Pearl Nash

Poppy Nwosu

The summer is finally here, and Pearl Nash is on a mission to save her slowly disintegrating friendship with a whirlwind end-of-year road trip that is definitely, absolutely, most positively going to solve all her problems.

Except, instead of her best friend Daisy's feet on her dash, suddenly Pearl ends up stuck in the middle of the desert beside Obi Okocha, a boy with a mega-watt smile and an endlessly irritating attitude. Tasked with delivering him to the most epic end-of-year party ever, located in a beach shack in literal middle-of-nowhere woop woop, Pearl Nash is certain that nothing could be worse than this.

She's wrong.

Add in a breakdown, multiple arguments, an AWOL nana and a kiss that was most definitely a huge mistake, and suddenly Pearl has the perfect ingredients for the perfect disaster

Road Tripping with Pearl Nash is a story about home and family, about breaking apart and fusing together, and, of course, about love.

Making Friends with Alice Dyson

Poppy Nwosu

Alice Dyson knows exactly how she'll be spending her final year of high school: with her head down, concentrating on her textbooks and homework. She's focused on the future, and nothing is going to get in her way.

Until a bizarre encounter with the school's most notorious troublemaker derails all her plans, turning Alice into the unwilling centre of attention and her life into one enormous complication.

And even worse? Now Teddy Taualai won't leave her alone.

A romantic story about rumours, friendship, and discovering who you really are.

Taking Down Evelyn Tait

Poppy Nwosu

Impulsive Lottie – heavy-metal fan, expert tomato-grower and frequent visitor to the principal's office – is in even more trouble than usual.

Her best friend Grace has dropped an unlikely bombshell: she's dating Lottie's mortal enemy, good-girl Evelyn Tait.

Studious Jude, the boy next door, has the perfect war plan. Lottie will beat Evelyn at her own good-girl game, unveiling Miss Perfect's sinister side in the process.

Taking life more seriously starts as fun, but soon offers its own rewards . . . so long as Lottie can manage gorgeous Sebastian's sudden interest, Jude acting weird, and the discovery that she might actually be good at something.

Taking Down Evelyn Tait is a story about family, friends and embracing who you are. Even if that person is kind of weird.

Trouble is my Business
Lisa Walker

Olivia Grace, recently retired teen PI, has her priorities sorted. Pass first-year law, look after her little sister, and persuade her parents to come back from a Nepali monastery to resume . . . well, parenting. But after Olivia's friend Abbey goes missing in Byron Bay, a short drive from Olivia's Gold Coast home, she can't sit back and study Torts. It's time to go undercover as hippie-chick Nansea, in hippie-chic Byron Bay, hub of influencers and international tourism, and home of yoga, surfing and wellness culture.

The Girl with the Gold Bikini
Lisa Walker

Eighteen-year-old Olivia Grace has deferred her law degree and ducked out of her friends' gap-year tour of Asia. Instead, she's fulfilling her childhood dream of becoming a private investigator, following in the footsteps of Nancy Drew and Veronica Mars – who taught her everything she knows, including a solid line in quick-quipping repartee, the importance of a handbag full of disguises, and a way of mixing business with inconvenient chemistry.

Playing Watson to the Sherlock of her childhood friend, detective agency owner Rosco (once the Han Solo to her Princess Leia), Olivia pursues a routine cheating husband case from the glitzy Gold Coast to Insta-perfect Byron Bay, where she faces yoga wars, dirty whale activism, and a guru who's kind of a creep.

Olivia Grace is a teenage screwball hercine for the #metoo era, and *The Girl with the Gold Bikini* is a body-positive detective romp, rich with pop-culture pleasures.

Wakefield Press is an independent publishing and
distribution company based in Adelaide, South Australia.
We love good stories and publish beautiful books.
To see our full range of books, please visit our website at
www.wakefieldpress.com.au
where all titles are available for purchase.
To keep up with our latest releases, news and events,
subscribe to our monthly newsletter.

Find us!

Facebook: www.facebook.com/wakefield.press
Twitter: www.twitter.com/wakefieldpress
Instagram: www.instagram.com/wakefieldpress